Exposure

Kolleen Fraser

HOT TREE PUBLISHING

For information, contact the publisher, Hot Tree Publishing.

www.hottreepublishing.com

Editing: Hot Tree Editing

Cover Designer: BookSmith Design

E-book ISBN: 978-1-922359-29-2

Paperback ISBN: 978-1-922359-30-8

ONE

I STARE AT THE PHONE BOOTH IN FRONT OF ME WITH its dirty, graffitied walls and foul stench. I could call. No one is watching as I nervously glance left to right, expecting someone to stop me. No one ever watches me. The helpline number I hastily wrote on my hand during study hall burns with possibility. I wonder what would happen if I called. Would the police come crashing through the door like knights in shining armor, ready to save the poor damsel? Or would they send a caseworker to look down on us and tear me and my brother apart?

I used to wonder why kids were taken away from their families. My family is a hot mess of dysfunction, but I always thought if I kept my head down, I would be okay.

But standing here now, a tattered sundress weighing heavily in my backpack, I understand why kids need protection, why I have every reason to call for help. But in my experience, no one cares if a child is broken.

I walk past the phone booth, leaving any hopes of a new life behind me as I reluctantly trudge home.

I have a roof over my head and manage to eat at least one meal a day; I'm surviving just fine. I never used to daydream about running away; now I choke back tears at the very thought of stepping foot in our apartment. I can't go home. I collapse against the side of a building in the throes of another panic attack. They've been happening a lot lately. Gasping like a fish out of water, I reach for the one thing that will make it all stop. Ripping the pin off my bag—the "No Means No" written in bold mocking me—I open it and drag the sharp metal across my forearm once, then again. I watch as the two angry red lines dot with blood. As the world slows and my heart beats loudly in my ears, I let out a calming breath, and my whole body relaxes against the building. A group of teens passing stares at me in disgust, calling me a freak. They aren't wrong. I don't know when cutting became my release. I like the way it makes me feel in control. It calms me in a way nothing else can.

I could stay with friends, if I had any, to avoid going home. But even if I wasn't a social outcast, I'd still have to go home sometime.

I've stopped trying to fit in at school. Mostly because I prefer to be invisible. And then there's the fact that I don't have a cell phone, a car, a promising future, or parents who give a shit at home.

After spending a few nights sleeping in phone booths and bathroom stalls, you'd think someone would have come looking for me. The truth is, no one notices when I reluctantly drag myself back through the door.

I find the apartment exactly as I left it: beer cans on the floor, dirty dishes stacked and rotting in the sink. Home sweet home. Puke-yellow shag carpeting has seen better decades, and the green appliances have sat unused and filthy since we moved in a few years ago. The couch—ripped to within an inch of its life—smells of piss and puke. This apartment hasn't been updated since the seventies, I guarantee it. It's filthy, and I don't mean the dust bunnies and moldy dishes.

I can't seem to see past these four dirty walls. I used to daydream about escaping to some wonderful existence; now I don't bother trying to grab at something that will always be out of reach. Outside these filthy walls is a filthy apartment building surrounded by a filthy neighborhood. There's no end to it.

A wave of nausea runs over me as I stand in the doorway. I should have called the help line. But I know better. Sure, they'd take me away from this hell, but then they'd put me in foster care, and I can't leave my older brother, Matty.

We survived our childhood by having each other's backs. He's stood in front of me and taken a beating more times than I can remember.

My mother, who demands we call her Erica, has an attraction to a certain kind of man. If my father was anything like the parade of angry losers she hooks up with, I'm happy I never met him. Ron is the worst one so far. Whenever he's in the apartment, I walk on eggshells, trying to be invisible, to not wake up his dark side or draw his eyes to me. Erica gets mad as a snake when she catches him watching me, though usually it's just a quick slap across the face.

That, I can take.

The last time it happened, she beat me unconscious, screaming something about whoring myself in front of him. I try to avoid the apartment when the two of them are here, especially if they're drinking or high, which is pretty much all the time.

I thought I was home alone that day—the one when he walked in on me in the bathroom. I was admiring how pretty the yellow dress was; I'd stolen it out of the lost-and-found box at school. Turning side to side like I was six, not sixteen, I watched the dress swirl around me. I'd never felt so beautiful.

The moment his predatory gaze caught mine in the mirror's reflection, I knew he wasn't going to let me walk away.

TODAY THE WALLS FEEL LIKE THEY'RE CLOSING IN ON me. I don't want to be here, but there's nowhere else to go. Erica doesn't usually wake up before noon, so I have a few hours before she's conscious. As a child, I remember curling myself behind her still body. That was as motherly as Erica Young ever got. A poor unloved child clinging to her comatose mother until her heart stopped aching with loneliness. Now she rarely speaks to me. If I try to talk to her, she snaps at me, asking where Matthew is.

Someday I'll see the world outside this shitty

apartment. Dip my toes into the ocean's clear blue water, rinsing the filth imbedded in my soul. The closest thing I've got to a savior is my brother, Matty. He watches out for me, and I watch out for him, as much as he'll let me. He's so protective of me.

I step over another discarded beer bottle on my way to my bedroom. From the hall, I catch my reflection in the bathroom mirror and flinch. How can I appear the same on the outside when I feel completely different inside? My body has healed, but nothing will change the ugliness that has now tainted me.

All because of a dress as bright as the sun. When I saw it in the lost-and-found at school, I couldn't stop myself from taking it. It made me feel carefree. It wasn't dirty or stained; it was the most beautiful thing I'd ever seen.

I'M POSING IN FRONT OF THE SINK, ADMIRING MYSELF IN the mirror when I see the reflection of him standing there, watching me.

"I'm all done," I say as I rush past him, but his dry, calloused fingers reach out, wrapping around my arm.

"Let me look at you. You're such a pretty little thing."

I back away from him until I hit the sink. I turn

around to avoid his eyes but see them in the mirror. He presses himself into my back, making me cringe away from his hardness.

"You like that, don't you, baby girl?" His breath stinks of cigarettes and whisky.

A whimper escapes me. "Don't touch me!" Anger raging through me, I slam my elbow back, trying to hit him, but I'm not strong enough. I resort to begging him to let me go.

"Shut up. You asked for this. You want it." His hand squeezing my throat turns my pleas into hoarse choking. My lungs feel like they're going to burst. I claw at his arm and beg—him, God, anyone—to please don't let this happen.

I fight him and scream for help, but nothing stops his hand from slipping under my dress, touching me in ways that will scar me forever. My eyes stay locked on the poor girl in the mirror, watching the tears stream from her scared eyes onto her attacker's choking hand. I hate her. I love her. I wish I knew how to save her.

Mother comes barreling in the room, screaming like a banshee, arms flailing madly. His assault stops abruptly as he takes a beating from Erica. Relief rushes through me at the thought of what could have happened.

But that relief is stunted as pain erupts across my scalp. Erica drags me by the hair out of the bathroom; I don't see where Ron ran off to. I hold on to her hand, trying in vain to lessen the pull on my scalp.

"You little slut. I knew it was only a matter of time before this happened," she curses, tossing me to the floor.

"I... I didn't do anything. He... he hurt me." I barely choke out the horrible words over the sobs coming out of me.

She stands silent, just staring at me. Her eyes are glossed over, but the glare is piercing. Her slap has such force that I'm shaken; my legs give out, and I crumple to the floor.

"You little whore. You think you're so grown up you can take my man? I'm done with both of you. You have held me back my whole life, ruined every good thing I ever had," she screams at me before storming into her room. She comes out with a bag over her shoulder. "I should have aborted you when I had the chance. You're both useless weights dragging me down. Well, not anymore. I'm gone." She walks out, the door slamming behind her.

She can't mean it. She's just mad. She'll be back.

I curl into a ball, cradling my burning cheek. My new summer dress is now ripped and stained with blood.

THE DRESS I STILL CARRY IN MY BACKPACK.

The bruises are still prominent on my arm. His

fingers dug so deep I thought I would bleed. The sounds of that day still echo through this small dingy room. I shake my head, trying to erase the memory.

Placing my bag on my bed, I glance across the room at Matty's empty bed. Sharing a bedroom with my brother would be awkward if he were ever here. He avoids this place as much as I do, but I appreciate the lock he installed on our bedroom door for my protection. I can't bear the thought of telling him what happened. I can still feel where Ron put his hands on me. His unwanted touch has changed me from the innocent girl I was just a week ago.

Matty'll blame himself for leaving me unprotected, I know it. Or worse, he'll blame me, like Erica did.

I wonder if she would ever really leave us.

Blindly grabbing my beloved pins off my bag before sitting on the floor, I drag the pin slowly across my skin, leaving a satisfying pink line trailing across my forearm. Right next to the others but not as deep this time; a ladder of angry lines all at different stages of healing. Proof of my weakness, proof of what I do to survive, the high price of my sanity. I should press a little harder, find something sharper and end it all. I wouldn't have to face Ron when he and Erica come back—if they come back.

Droplets of blood decorate the thin line sporadically. I crave this release like a drug.

I've never tried to hide my cutting. I'm not suffering in silence; I'm screaming at the top of my lungs for someone to see me. To see the marks and take me away from this place, make me whole. I'm sure people see the bruises, scars, and cuts marring my too-skinny frame, my messy brown hair rarely washed, and sad dark eyes. I suppose I might be considered pretty if I put a little effort in, wash my hair, and wear clean clothes, but being beautiful seems like a curse; it draws unwanted attention. I want to be invisible. I never want a man to look at me and think he can touch me without permission. I want to feel safe, to be stronger than I am.

Honestly, I don't know what I would say if someone offered help. In this moment, when my whole body hums and relaxes with this new pain, they could offer refuge, but I would choose my pain over their solutions. This is the only way I feel alive. If I can control my pain, they can't control me.

THE FRONT DOOR SLAMMING SHUT WAKES ME, AND I cringe at who it could be. Steps approach, and then

I'm lifted off the ground by familiar arms. Matty has hold of me.

"What happened, Lex?" he asks as he lays me on my bed and brushes my hair away from the injured side of my face.

"I just wanted it to stop. I thought she would make him leave so he wouldn't hurt me again. She didn't believe me. She called me a whore, Matty." I give in to the uncontrollable sobs.

My brother's warm, comforting arms envelop me. This is the only safe place in my whole world.

"What are you talking about? Where have you been, Alexa? Who hurt you?" he asks as I cling to him, too terrified to speak.

"I couldn't stay here, Matty. He cornered me in the bathroom. He... touched me," I whisper, afraid he too will hate me for it.

His body goes rigid, and he pulls away from me. "What? I'll fucking kill him!" Tortured eyes on mine, he searches for answers.

"I'm so sorry, Matty. I begged him to stop. I tried to fight, but I couldn't. Then Mom came home, and she made him stop, but she was so mad. I think she left us. I'm so sorry."

I grab at his shirt as he gets up and starts pacing.

"Fuck! I hate this fucking place!" he screams to the universe.

I walk over to him, begging, "I'm sorry. Please don't be mad at me!"

He stops pacing and takes me in his arms, squeezing me so tight. "You did *nothing wrong*, Lexi." He pulls back and meets my eyes. "You hear me? None of this is your fault. I'm sorry I wasn't here to protect you." Tears form in his eyes as he hugs me again. "She's not going anywhere, Lex. I swear to you, I'll kill them both if she lets him back in the door."

I hold him close. I can never lose him. He's the only good thing I have left in the whole miserable world.

TWO

ERICA ISN'T HOME WHEN I GET HOME FROM SCHOOL, which means she's probably left us for good. Her bed is empty. I ignore the dread building in the pit of my stomach and check her closet and dresser. Both are empty; she took everything. I run from her room through the house, searching for anything that belongs to her. It's all gone. She's really left us this time.

My whole world is crumbling to dust.

I slip to the ground, blankly staring at the front door. Everything keeps piling up on me—the hatred, the anger. The whole world has finally succeeded at breaking me. I've been through a lot in my life and come out kicking, but this is too much. What are we going to do?

This life is too raw, too painful. Just breathing in and out is too hard.

Fuck this life. Fuck this white trash black hole of an existence I was handed.

I start screaming. Smashing everything that will break. Fuck it all.

Matty comes home late at night. I haven't moved, haven't eaten—not that the barren cupboards have food anyway. He has blood on his shirt; he's been fighting again. I overheard some neighborhood kids saying he fights for money.

His eyes are dark and filled with pain when they land on me.

"What the fuck happened here? Where's Erica?" he asks, surveying the carnage.

"She came and took all her stuff while I was at school. She left. I don't think she's coming back this time." The words make it all too real, and I collapse forward and cry into my hands.

He disappears into her room, and I hear him cursing as he discovers her things gone. I just sit here, staring off, completely lost. What will happen to us now?

"She picked him over us, and it's my fault. I'm sorry," I sob as he walks back to me.

"Stop crying. Don't you shed one tear for either of those lowlifes."

"She might come back."

"Don't be stupid, Lex. She isn't coming back. We have to leave."

"Leave? Where?"

"She's a couple months behind in rent, and we can't pay, so we've got to get out of here before they come collecting. They'll bring CPS with them and separate us. We'll end up in foster care."

"You don't know that. Maybe they won't separate us."

"Of course they will. But I'm almost eighteen. I can take care of us."

A shiver runs through my body. I try to lock my fear away, to see this as a blessing. She'll never hurt me again.

We pack our meager belongings and run through the back streets in the shadows away from the apartment. This is it, we're on our own now. The full moon lights up the dark night with a silvery glow. Everything is happening so fast.

"Where are we supposed to go, Matty?" Fresh tears stream down my cold cheeks. "What are we going to do for money?" I finally ask. "How long can we keep running? We're just kids. Where will we live?"

"Jesus, enough questions. I'm sorry, Lex, but this is the only way we can stay together."

I start shaking my head, pleading with him. "Please, Matty. Maybe it won't be so bad if we just go home," I croak, lip quivering, clutching his coat.

His words come out hard and with an edge. "There's no home to go back to. Do you want to never see me again? You want to end up in some foster home that'll be just like living with Mom? I can take care of us better than she ever could."

His strong voice penetrates to my bones. My eyes fill with tears.

He's right. This is the only way.

"We'll take care of each other. Like always," I offer with a small smile.

He pulls me into his arms and kisses the top of my head. "Always."

THREE

I'M CURLED INTO MYSELF ON THE SEAT OF A PICKUP truck Matty stole, watching the desert whip by under the light of the moon. The events of the last twenty-four hours disappear in a cloud of dust behind us.

"Where'd you learn to steal a car?" What kind of trouble has he been getting into?

He doesn't answer me, just grips the steering wheel, staring straight ahead. I can see his frustration setting in as he drives.

I know I shouldn't smile, but the thought of never going back to that place makes my heart feel lighter. Hope stretches out in front of us with endless possibilities.

THE REALITY OF BEING A RUNAWAY MEANS WE CAN'T afford an apartment let alone food. We ditched the truck a few blocks back and are on foot once again.

"My friend Jax lives nearby. He said we could stay with him until I find a job and a place for us to live."

I nod in agreement, even though he isn't looking at me. At this point I have no choice but to follow him wherever he thinks is best.

Long before the row of townhouses comes into view, the beats thumping through the neighborhood can be heard. So much for the quiet night I was hoping for.

I follow Matty closely as he enters the building and climbs the stairs toward what I assume is the living area. With each step, the music gets louder. I can feel it pulsing in my chest. I'm surprised the police haven't shown up to tell them to keep quiet.

Meandering through the maze of people, Matty waves to a guy playing beer pong. He lifts his chin in response and motions for us to follow. Once outside, it's quiet enough to talk, if only my ears would stop ringing.

"Hey, man, you made good time. Run into any trouble?" Jax stands at an intimidating six feet tall with tattoos and bulging muscles, but his smile is kind.

"Nah, coast was clear. You sure it's okay for us to stay?"

"Of course. It's not always this crazy, I promise. This must be your sister, Alexa," he says, reaching out a hand to me. I turn to Matty for reassurance before I shake this stranger's hand.

"Well, all right, then. I'll show you where you'll be staying." We follow him back through the party and into a small room with two beds. "Y'all can stay here rent free for a month. Sorry I can't offer more, but my roommate will be back next month. I'm sure you can get yourselves settled somewhere by then."

"Thanks, man. We appreciate it," Matty offers.

Jax contemplates a moment before saying, "This door has a lock. Use it. No one is going to hurt you, but you don't want anyone coming in here to pass out or fuck."

His words take me by surprise, but I give him a quick nod, my eyes wide.

Matty gives my shoulder a squeeze. "It's been a long day. Try to get some sleep, okay?"

"Okay. Good night, and thank you, Jax."

I lock the door quickly behind their retreating backs and lie on top of the blankets to stare at the ceiling. The beat thumps in rhythm with my racing heart.

I toss and turn for a while, but sleep won't find me. I reluctantly get out of bed, grab a sweater, and decide a little fresh air might help, So I push my way through the party and out the front door. No one bothers me; if there is one thing I know how to do, it's be invisible.

The air is warm even in the middle of the night; summer is here, and in southern California, it doesn't ever really leave, it just gets unbearable. I sit on the front steps, arms wrapped around my knees, and try to make sense of the last month.

The door opening behind me snaps me out of my daydream. I glance up to see a guy in a ball cap and hoodie lighting a cigarette.

Spotting me a few feet away, he lifts his chin in greeting. "You all right?"

I nod. "Just getting some fresh air."

He waves his cigarette at me. "I guess I just wrecked that for you." He walks down the steps and stands a good six feet away, keeping his smoke downwind.

That tiny act of kindness makes me smile. "Thank you."

"It's not real safe sitting out here alone. Do you

need a ride home or something?" he asks, blowing out a halo of smoke that slowly floats up and disappears into the stars above.

I laugh. "I am home, I guess. I'm living here temporarily. And anyway, I'm not alone. You're here. You can protect me."

"And how do you know I'm not a bad guy?"

"Trust me, I know bad guys, and you're not one of them."

He tilts his head, pondering that statement. "How did you end up living with Jax?"

I shrug. "No freaking idea. It's my first night here. He's a friend of my brother. It's only for a month, until we can find a place."

"Where're your parents?"

"Parents bailed, so it's just us now. You ask a lot of questions for a sexy stranger in the dark." I laugh.

"Sexy, huh?" he asks with a smile.

"Oh crap, I said that out loud? I must be tired." I called him sexy to his face. Lord, let the earth swallow me now.

He sits down next to me. Holding his hand out, he says, "Noah King, AKA sexy stranger in the dark."

I smile up at him, extending my hand. "Lexi Young, hot mess on a step."

He chuckles at this, and his laugh makes my heart happy. What is happening to me?

A Jeep pulls up in front of us and honks. He gives them a quick wave before turning back to me.

Without thought or reasoning, I use his shirt to pull him closer, and our lips meet in the most perfect kiss that has ever existed. I want to own this moment, to take charge and prove to myself that I can still be normal. I can kiss a boy I think is cute. I'm not completely broken.

He cradles my face, and the kiss deepens passionately. He pulls back, smiles, and places one more delicate kiss on my lips and one on my forehead before stepping away. "That was…," he starts.

"My first kiss," I finish with a smile.

"I've never been anyone's first kiss. I'm honored." Taking my hand, he places one perfect kiss on my palm. "Stay safe, Lexi Young, hot mess on a step."

I revel in his attention and the zing going through my body at his touch. "I'll do my best, Noah King, sexy stranger in the dark."

He waves and jumps in the back of the Jeep, disappearing down the street.

I go up to my room, hoping sleep finds me, but instead I spend most of the night trying to calm my erratic heartbeat.

I WAKE UP EARLY THE NEXT MORNING AND MAKE MY way to the bathroom. A girl is passed out in the tub. I shake her arm, trying to wake her, but there is no way she's moving. Great. I pull the shower curtain closed to get a little privacy while I take care of business.

I can't believe I kissed a random guy last night. What was I thinking? I was thinking Noah King was the cutest, sweetest guy to ever talk to me, and I wanted him to be my first kiss.

While washing my hands and face, trying to avoid my reflection in the mirror as always, my eyes land on a razor blade propped against the vanity. I gasp out loud with the sudden and overwhelming need to cut, to drag that blade across my skin in sweet release. I've never seen a razor blade before; I cut with whatever I can find, usually a pin from my bag. When I touch the shiny, cold blade, my hands immediately start shaking.

I want to stop, I really do. I don't want to be this weak person whose first instinct is to hurt herself, but I'm helpless against this. Pulling my sleeve up, I start a new line next to the others.

I'm almost finished when the bathroom door

swings open without warning. I look up in horror as Jax stares at my bleeding arm with wide eyes.

"The fuck? Matt, your sister is trying to kill herself in my fucking bathroom!"

I'm mortified, utterly mortified. I jerk my sleeve down and push past him, bolting to my room.

An argument breaks out between the two of them, but the buzzing in my body drowns them out. I flip the lock on the door behind me. I can't believe I got caught. I never get caught. I'm always so careful.

Matty is banging on the door hard enough to make the wood vibrate. "Open this fucking door, Alexa. I swear to God, I will break it down if you don't open it in the next five seconds. I'll pay you for a new door, asshole," he yells at Jax when he protests.

"Okay!" I shout, unlocking the door before climbing back on the bed, hiding my face.

"What the hell, Lexi," he says as he comes in, closing the door behind him. The bed dips with Matty's weight and he pulls at my sleeve, revealing the recent wounds and many old scars I've carved into my flesh. He gasps at the sight of them, and his grip tightens around my wrist. "I thought you stopped. You promised me you'd stopped."

"I don't know what I was thinking. I don't do it

that often, really," I offer as an excuse, pulling my sleeve down over the offending marks.

"Bullshit. Look at what you've done to yourself. Why, Lex?"

"Are you fucking kidding? Mom abandoned us, leaving us homeless because her boyfriend tried to rape me. Do you have any idea how messed up that is? This is it, Matthew. Welcome to my rock bottom." I say his full name with venom, like Erica used to. It'll hit a nerve, and in this moment, I want to hurt him. Raising my arm, I motion to the scars, furious. I want to scream. "This is how I get through the day. Both of us hurt ourselves to dull the pain. You fight, I cut. You've got no right to judge me."

He stares at me, eyes full of shock. Guilt starts eating away at me for lashing out at him. He needs to realize not everything can be fixed; some things are broken beyond repair.

After that awful scene, Jax pushes for us to leave. He doesn't want some girl offing herself in his bathroom. I don't blame him.

It takes Matty a few days to find us a small apartment. We would be on the streets if it wasn't for the money he brings in—illegally, I assume. All of this is falling on Matty, hard. The stress is showing in the dark circles under his eyes and the defeated slump in his shoulders. I wish I could help, but in truth, I'm the root to all this evil. My actions have landed us in this mess, not his.

The apartment is small for a two-bedroom, with little more than a kitchen and a couch, but even this has to be more than he can afford. Though he doesn't tell me anything about how much money he makes or what he does to earn it I take my meager belongings and sit on my bed with them, trying to feel comfortable here. This is home now, I guess.

After a week in our new place, I finally feel at home. But there's always that niggling thought that what he's doing for money is probably illegal, not to mention dangerous. I see him getting ready to leave for work, and while he won't tell me where it is, I know he'll do anything to keep us here. Which makes me worry even more.

"You're not doing anything stupid, are you?"

He rolls his eyes at my question. "What I do is none of your business. Stay in the apartment, okay? This neighborhood sucks, and we don't need any more trouble." His words are impatient and sharp enough to cut me.

I nod. The last thing I need is for him to direct

his anger at me. "You'll come back, w-won't you?" I stammer, terrified of his answer.

He sighs, sitting beside me. "Of course I'm coming back, Lex. Why would you even think that?"

"You've been angry and distant. I'm sorry I got us into this mess. Maybe you don't want to be stuck with me anymore." I can't look at him as tears clog my throat.

He pulls me into a tight hug. "Alexa, I'll always come back. You and me, kid, we're forever. Nothing you do will ever push me away, you understand me? I will never leave you."

He pulls my chin up so he can see my eyes. I nod, smiling up at him. And just like that, the weight of the world is a little less.

Things get easier for us after that.

It's officially summer vacation, so the issue of finding a school can wait for fall. Whatever Matty is doing in his long hours away from home, he's making a lot of money. Our rent troubles are over, and we settle into our new lives. Sadly, I spend most of my time alone in the apartment, trying to not let my anxiety amp up into a panic attack. I used to be alone a lot and it never bothered me, but now my stress rises with every passerby and raised voices. I can't stay locked up in here, but the thought of leaving the apartment causes a cold sweat to erupt across my skin.

The apartment has two bedrooms and a small kitchen and living room. It's small, but since I'm here by myself all the time it feels almost too big. I putter around all day, cleaning and trying to keep myself busy, which is getting old real fast. I don't want to be a victim anymore. I want to feel strong, to be able to walk out that door and explore the city. I don't want to be broken. I don't want my life to be smaller, for me to be weaker because of it.

No, I'm a survivor. I won't shrink, I'll fight.

THE NEXT MORNING, AGAINST MY BETTER JUDGMENT, I pick a fight with a very tired and irritable Matty. "I can't sit in this apartment day in and day out. I'm going freaking crazy! Maybe you could teach me how to fight?"

"I don't have time to hold your fucking hand, Alexa. I've got shit to do."

"Well, good for you, Matty. I sit here with *nothing* to do all freaking day. What do I have to do before you'll let me go outside? If you won't teach me to fight back, I'll find someone who will. Nothing bad is going to happen to me." I make a scene of flipping through the Yellow Pages aggressively.

"Seriously, the Yellow Pages? You really want to learn to fight?"

"Yes! I hate this weakness in me. Being scared to leave the apartment. I need this."

He takes out his cell, holding a finger up to me when I try to talk. I try to listen in on his conversation with someone he called "Z-man."

The call ends as quickly as it started. Pulling me behind him, he walks us out of the apartment.

By the time we reach the sidewalk, I can't hold in my curiosity. "Where are we going?"

I find out soon enough. A block away from home, we stop in front of what looks like a warehouse. He opens the door, pulling me inside. It's a gym, a fighters' gym. There's a wall of treadmills on one end, but the rest of the vast space is full of men—all muscles and testosterone—punching bags, trainers, and each other.

I stare at him, confused. "Matty, what are we doing here? Is this where you train?"

"Matt, I told you, training teenage girls is not my style," a man says as he approaches us. He stands with his arms crossed over his chest, an intimidating wall of muscle towering over me. He's six feet tall and easily three times my size.

Matty can't be serious. This guy looks like he eats two of me for breakfast.

Matty pulls me toward this monster of a man. "Hey, Z, this is my kid sister, Alexa, the one I was telling you about. Just teach her self-defense or something. She spends too much time alone and keeps bitching about being able to explore or some shit. Can you teach her to kick some ass if she gets in a pinch?"

I just stare at my brother wide-eyed, my jaw dropping to the floor. Self-defense? I've never taken anything like that, but I must admit the idea of learning to defend myself and fight back ignites a flicker of hope somewhere inside me.

"Oh my God, Matty, seriously?" I squeal, bouncing up and down while squeezing his arm.

He's smiling at my excitement while the man known as Z seems a little scared, like he's never seen an excited teenage girl in his life and isn't quite sure how to deal.

"Dude, I want to help, I really do, but...," Upon seeing my smile drop, he adds, "Aww, hell, don't look at me like that, kid." He ponders something a moment. "Fine, you can come in the mornings and

I'll show her a few things. I'll let the guys know she'll be coming in and not to hassle her."

I launch at him, attempting to hug his massive body. Seriously, it's like hugging a brick wall; I barely get my hands to reach his shoulders. He steps back awkwardly. Excitement blooms in me, I can hardly contain it. "Thank you, Mr. Z. You won't regret it."

He just grumbles in response.

My eyes dance around the gym and its various equipment. "I feel stronger already."

I WAKE UP EARLY AND HEAD DOWN THE BLOCK TO THE gym. My stomach is dancing with butterflies as I open the door. I'm instantly hit with the smell of sweat, and I wrinkle my nose. Let's hope I get used to it. A dozen eyes are on me as I walk around searching for Z.

"Over here, Alexa." His gruff voice comes from a doorway across the room.

I step into his office, trying to ignore the curious eyes following me every step of the way. Z motions to a chair in front of his desk as I pass.

We sit staring at each other for a few seconds, and I shift my weight in the chair, uncomfortable with his scrutiny. Finally I break the silence. "There's a lot of guys out there. You think they'll be okay with me being here? I don't want to make anyone mad."

"It's my gym. I do whatever the fuck I want, and they can't do shit." I'm a bit taken aback by his statement; I thought the customer was always right. "What do you want out of your time here... Alexa, is it?"

"Lexi, please. Um... I guess I want to feel stronger, be able to defend myself if someone tries to... hurt me."

"You willing to do what I say with no bullshit arguments? I got no time for disrespectful teenagers."

"Of course. I'll follow orders. I'll show up on time and give it my all," I say with a little too much pep.

"You'll show up here every morning at seven o'clock, do the warm-up I assign you, and then I'll show you how to take down a man twice your size. Deal?"

I jump to my feet, extending my hand across his desk. "Deal! When do I start?"

"Now," he says, staring at my hand like it's a bag of poop. "Come on, I'll show you around."

Outside his office, the gym is buzzing with activity, and he silences them with a whistle that makes my eardrums rattle. "Listen up. This is Alexa. She'll be around the gym a couple mornings a week this summer." A few of the guys make crude comments and eye me up. "Show her some fucking respect! Alexa is sixteen years old. Do *not* give me a reason to kick your ass, understood?"

Their understanding echoes through the space.

I smile at Z. I like this guy; he's mean as hell but also sweet. Weird combo, but I dig it.

He sets me up in the corner, where I run on a treadmill for thirty minutes before he tells me to stop. I'm a gasping, sweaty mess; I'm not in horrible shape, but jogging thirty minutes is not something I'm used to.

"You need to build up your endurance. That's what the cardio is for. Now I need to see how you can throw a punch." Holding his padded hands up in front of him, he beckons me to attack him. "Go ahead, hit me."

I begin throwing punches. After each hit, he interrupts and corrects either my stance or my fists.

When our time is up, my whole body feels like a noodle. I can barely drag my butt back home. When I raise my arm in the shower, a whimper escapes me. But I vow to show up there until I'm stronger.

And I do just that.

For the next two weeks, he teaches me how to overpower someone coming at me and how to get away when being held down. He doesn't say, but I have a feeling Matty told him what happened to me. There is determination in his eyes, like he wants to make sure I'm never helpless again. He's a good guy, quiet, kind of mean, but deep down a giant teddy bear. The other guys in the gym don't bother me much; a few say hello when I come in, but mostly they mind their business and leave me to mine.

Three mornings a week, I'm at Z's mercy. I learn how to put enough weight behind a punch to cause damage, which for someone as small as I am is tricky. I'm a fast learner as it turns out.

Today as I leave, the front desk is empty, and the phone keeps ringing and ringing. I glance around; no one seems to notice or care, but I just can't leave it ringing. I pick it up and hope Z doesn't kill me.

"Good morning, Z's Gym," I say with as much authority as I can muster. Thankfully it's just a customer asking for the hours of operation, which are posted on the door, so I'm able to help quickly.

As I stand to leave, the phone rings again. With a sigh, I settle myself into the desk and answer the phone. I turn on the computer, and luckily their schedule and all the information I require is sitting there for me.

I hang up the fourth call of the morning to see Z standing in the doorway, arms crossed, watching me.

"Uh, sorry, Z. I know I shouldn't have done that, but there was no one here. Erica used to get so pissed when I would answer the collectors who would call our apartment, but I just can't let it ring, you know? Anyway, I better go. Here are your messages. See you tomorrow," I say in a rush, trying to get it all out quickly as he glances at the messages I handed him.

"Receptionist quit last week. Haven't had time to find a new one. You want the job?"

"A job? Here?" I question in disbelief. Why would he want me, some stupid kid, working here? "Okay!"

He seems surprised that I agreed, but he nods. "You can work out until nine and run the phones until five three days a week, as long as Matt's okay with you working here. Only until school starts. Talk it out with him and give me your answer tomorrow."

"It'll be fine, really. He won't care."

And just like that, I got a job answering phones at the reception desk a few days a week.

I practically run home, bursting through the door before I squeal in delight.

Best day ever.

———

MATTY AND I ARE ARGUING AGAIN. SEEMS LIKE ALL WE do is fight these days. I make him feel trapped, I know I do. He works all the time, doing God only knows what so we can eat and have a roof over our heads. I feel like a jerk saying it's not enough for me. I want to ask him for the freedom to go where I please. Seems like an easy thing, but when you were raised in the world Matty and I were, the idea of letting a teenage girl wander the streets alone is a scary thought.

"I can defend myself now. I've learned a lot. Trust me, it'll be okay." When he still doesn't agree, I bring out the big guns. "This is ridiculous! Most girls are free to wander around the city! Keeping me here is like torture!" I say, overexaggerating as only a teenage girl can. I know he'll cave. It's just a matter of time.

"Fine, you can go exploring. Just wait until I get you a cell, okay? That way if you get in trouble, I can come get you."

I nod, excited. "Um… could I maybe get a camera too? Like a real camera, Matty?" I feel bad asking him to spend his money on something special just for me, but I would be saving for years if I had to pay for it with my own money.

He smiles, knowing I've always wanted a camera. He messes up my hair and says, "Yeah, kid, I can get you a *real* camera. Anything you want." He hugs me close.

I'm so lucky to have him. Best brother ever.

True to his word, he gets me a camera, a cell phone, and a laptop. I'd say he bought them, but I assume he stole them or bought them from someone who'd stolen them. I'm too excited to care. He also leaves me an allowance on the kitchen counter for whatever I might need while he's away. The possibilities are endless; I could get my own food, go to the movies, go shopping. I've never gone shopping for clothes anywhere but the thrift shop, and I've never gone to a movie theatre.

My happiness at the possibilities is dulled by the small voice in the back of my mind wondering where the money is coming from. I just hope whatever he's doing, he's being safe.

I play with my new camera for two days straight, even bringing it to Z's with me. I spend most of my shift poring over as much of the manual as my brain can take. I snap hundreds of pictures inside the apartment, the gym, and anything that piques my interest on my walk to and from work. Watching how the light and shadows change in each setting, I'm entranced.

Tomorrow is my day off, and the day I leave this apartment to explore the city on my own. I open my laptop and search out maps and places to go. I can barely sleep with the excitement of what I'll see.

FOUR

I WAKE UP EARLY, SHOWER, AND GET READY TO GO. With my camera around my neck, I step out into the sunny morning. Seeing the world anew through the lens.

After I wander around the city for a couple hours, I make my way to the skate park I found online. There are kids my age everywhere. Here, I'm not a runaway from a broken home. I'm just a regular kid hanging out with other regular kids on a lazy summer day. I sit on one of the benches and watch the skateboarders do their gravity-defying tricks. Lifting my camera, I start snapping pictures of everyone and everything. I want so badly to get closer. I bet if I lay on the ground while they jumped over me it would make an incredible picture. I wish I had the nerve to ask one of them; making friends was never my strong suit.

A girl starts walking toward me, watching me curiously with her bright blue eyes. I must seem kind of crazy sitting here taking pictures like I'm the paparazzi. I smile politely at her as she sits next to me. She's pretty in an almost angelic way, with long pale yellow hair framing her face, then falling down her back in waves. She's stunning, and her smile is warm and friendly. I decide right then that I like this girl.

"Hi, I'm Elise. Do you go to West High? You don't look familiar. Have you been here before?" she asks with a smile, tucking her flyaway hair behind her ear.

"Um… no. I just moved here, so I don't know which school I'm supposed to go to. I'm Lexi." I return her smile.

"Oh cool. So you like to take pictures, huh?"

"I do, yeah," I say, beaming. "My brother got this for me. Today is the first day I've had off since I got it, so I'm trying it out. Wish I could get closer to the action though." I point at the skaters, explaining the angles I want to shoot from.

"That would be so cool!" She stands up, searching

the crowd. "Marco!" she calls out, when nothing happens, she does it again, "Marco!"

"Polo?" I ask with a giggle, standing up next to her.

She falls against me, laughing so hard she snorts, which sets us off laughing again.

"Oh my God, I can't believe I never thought of that before! I must look insane. I'm always yelling at Marco."

"Who's Marco?"

"My husband. He's here somewhere skating or eating. You know guys, it's either sex, food, or skating." She laughs it off.

Husband? She seems way too young to be married.

"No, not really. I mean, I don't... talk to guys. I mean, I talk to my brother and to Z, but they aren't guys, they're like grown men. I've never... I mean, I don't...." I cringe, turning away. I don't want to talk about my inexperience with guys.

"Hey, it's okay. I shouldn't run off at the mouth like that. It's better to wait for someone you love," she reassures me with a smile.

"I agree. I think if you love someone, it's okay. I mean, I don't sleep around or anything. It's just... I was attacked by my mom's boyfriend, so I avoid putting myself in situations that are dangerous. Anyway, Matty doesn't let guys talk to me. Doesn't let me out of his sight really. He worries too much. If it weren't for Z, he would keep me locked away from the big bad world. Today was a big deal for him… and me." I finally manage to stop talking. I can't believe I dumped all that on her; she's going to run a mile to get away from the crazy chick with the camera.

Her smile disappears and her eyes gloss with tears as she processes my word vomit.

"Oh, Lexi, I'm so sorry," she says, hugging me. It's an odd thing to be hugged by a stranger.

"No, I'm sorry. I don't know why I told you all that. It's okay. I mean, obviously it's not okay, but it happened, and I can't change it. Matty is the only one who knows, though I think he told Z. Anyway, I can't seem to stop talking. I'm sorry, I must look insane," I ramble, shaking my head. I must be lonelier than I thought if I tell my life story to the first girl to speak to me.

"Hey, it's okay. We all have our stories. We all have these dark things trying to pull us under. Trick is to fill your life with things that make you snort-laugh. Then the hard days don't seem so bad. You're lucky to have your brother watching out for you." She flashes me a smile I return. She's awesome.

"You hollered for me like a crazy person, Your Majesty?" A tall, tatted-up guy walks up to us, rolling his eyes and bowing, watching our exchange with curiosity.

"Yes!" she declares with an exasperated sigh. "Like a hundred hours ago! Marco, love of my life, meet my new best friend, Lexi. Lexi, meet the love of my life, the man of my dreams, Marco." She waves her hand back and forth between us.

I reach out to shake his hand. He smirks at me curiously but shakes my hand.

"Nice to meet you, Lexi. What brings you to the park today?"

"Oh!" Elise yells, slapping him on the arm. "That's why I called you over! She's a photographer. Isn't that cool! She wanted to get closer shots of some of you guys in action. Think you can help her out?"

He rubs his arm where she smacked him. "For you, my wife, anything. Let me go ask a few guys and we'll call you over," he replies before kissing her on the cheek.

"Wife? That's cute," I say once Marco walks away.

She holds up her hand, showing me her wedding band. "Oh, it's for real. We did it a few months ago, right after I turned eighteen. We are blissfully in the honeymoon phase." She sighs, smiling toward where Marco is talking to some friends. "I know it probably seems crazy, but I've loved him my whole life. We don't have much family except each other, and Noah of course."

"It sounds like a fairy tale. It's sweet." Then my brain catches up. "Who's Noah?" I ask, thinking about that cute guy I met at Jax's place.

"Noah's my little brother and Marco's best friend. We're the three musketeers, have been since forever." She points to the guy talking to Marco.

Holy crap, it *is* the guy from Jax's house! Oh Lord, I feel my face flush. I can't stop staring at him. He's so gorgeous my stomach flips.

He glances over our way. We lock eyes, and he smiles when he sees me. I look away.

"Oh God. I should probably just go home. I don't know how to do this," I say to myself and turn to grab my bag.

"Do what?" she asks, touching my shoulder.

I suddenly feel so exposed out here, second-guessing the shorts I'm wearing. It's too much skin. I don't want to seem slutty.

"I kissed Noah at a party. I've never done anything like that before. I don't know how to talk to guys like him, he was so sweet. I thought I was being brave, but now I feel like an idiot," I babble, glancing over my shoulder. Oh God, they're coming this way. "He's just so damn cute, so I caved and kissed him. I never thought I would see him again. He probably thinks I'm a crazy stalker." My panic is evident in my trembling hands.

Elise just stands there listening to me until I stop my rambling. "Okay, settle down. We just met and you're already one of my favorite people ever. You know, he told me about a girl he met at Jax's party. He couldn't stop talking about you. Noah would never say or do anything to hurt you, that I can promise you. It'll be fine."

"Are you sure?"

"Yes. I've already adopted you into my family. Wanna know a secret?" she asks, and I nod. She leans in and whispers in my ear, "I'm pregnant." My eyes bug out and she laughs, bumping shoulders with me. "Now you've got to be my best friend because Lord knows I'll need help raising this baby," she confesses holding her flat stomach.

Marco and Noah are talking and laughing, his easy smile lighting up his face, and I watch him walk toward me, the way he moves, the way his muscles shift under his shirt. I've seen hot guys before, but none have shaken me up the way Noah does. It's scary and yet exciting.

I look away, staring at the ground. My body is a traitor.

"Noah, this is Lexi, but I'm guessing you already know that?" Elise says with a wink.

Marco shifts his gaze between us, confused. "You know each other?"

"She's the girl from the party!" Elise bursts out, causing my whole body to flush with embarrassment.

"No way."

"I know, right! It's like destiny."

"Shut up, Elise." Noah scratches the back of his neck nervously. "I went back to Jax's, but tragically, there were no hot messes on the step."

"Noah King, don't you dare call my new best friend a hot mess." Elise gasps, clearly outraged by his words, not getting our inside joke.

I smile at the memory of that night. "We had to move out a little earlier than planned."

"Yeah, I heard that."

My eyes shoot to his, which are staring down at my covered wrists. He knows. Jax must have told him about the "suicidal" girl he found in his bathroom. I shift awkwardly, wishing the earth would open and swallow me whole.

"Anyway, can she take some pictures of you guys doing jumps and stuff?" Elise asks, nudging my shoulder. "Right, Lexi?"

I nod, freaking out inside. Maybe it'll be easier to face him with a camera between us.

I take a deep breath and look up. He's gorgeous and intimidating, as perfect as I remembered, standing almost a foot taller than me with a lean, muscled build. His eyes, which seemed black the night we met, are now a deep dark brown and are staring right at me. A small smile tugs at the corner of his perfect kissable mouth.

"Um, yeah," I say. The world's most eloquent speaker, ladies and gentlemen.

Without saying a word, Noah reaches out to take my hand. It's like the earth shifts on its axis and my soul feels grounded, magical. We just stand there holding hands. I wonder if he feels it too.

I can't stop staring at him. I had convinced myself that he wasn't real, that I had dreamed it all. Yet here he is right in front of me, in the flesh. And he's holding my hand.

"Okay, guys? Could you ease up on the eye banging? There are children present." Elise laughs, holding a hand over her nonexistent baby bump. Her words are enough to snap us out of whatever that was.

"Would you mind if I take some pictures of you? I mean you guys." My cheeks heat with Noah's eyes on me.

"Yes, sounds fun. Let's do this!" He claps his hands together. He and Marco walk in front of us, laughing and pushing at each other.

Elise locks arms with me. "That was one hell of a second meeting, Miss Lexi. I wish I'd caught the first. What on earth were you doing living with Jax?" she asks, wrinkling her nose.

I smile back. "He let my brother and I stay there until we found a place. Noah was really nice to me on a night when I really needed it," I say with a shrug. "It felt so strange, like we were in a bubble and the whole world fell away. Is that normal?" I love that I finally have someone to ask about these things.

"Normal, no, but real and amazing and worth holding onto with both hands? Hell yes."

The guys lead us to a less populated area where they can skate around while I sit on the edge and snap pictures. Skating around shirtless, I'm surprised at how many tattoos they have for being fresh out of high school. I take a dozen pictures from all angles until the sun dips low in the sky.

"We're going to grab some food. Wanna come with us, Lexi?" Elise asks.

I smile. "Love to. All I have waiting for me at home is an empty apartment."

We walk a few blocks to a pizza place. It smells amazing. We sit in a booth while the guys place the order and return with our drinks. When Noah sits beside me, I think my heart is going to explode. His leg presses against mine for a moment, skin against skin, and my heart nearly leaps out of my chest.

Needing a distraction, I take out my camera and start flipping through the shots I took. Noah leans closer so he can see. His shoulder is against mine, his breath a whisper on my cheek. My breath hitches when I meet his eyes. We're only inches apart. I lose the nerve to hold eye contact and watch his lips, licking mine unconsciously.

"I like that one," he says, nodding toward the picture displayed on my camera screen. His breath sends a shiver across my neck.

"Me too, but this one—" I flick through the shots, finding the one of him with the sun turning him into a silhouette. "—is my favorite," I say, turning toward him. Whoa. This close, I can see the flecks of bronze in his dark eyes.

"I'm your favorite, hey?" he asks with a cheeky smile, nudging my shoulder. Looking up at him, I nod. "Check these out, Marco. She makes us look legit."

I pass the camera over so they can look through.

"You're pretty good with that thing," Marco comments.

"Thank you. It's what I want to be when I grow up," I say with a smile, then realize how stupid that sounds. I feel my cheeks flush. "I mean, I really like it."

"That's awesome! Marco and I are going to have our own tattoo shop. We're pretty good. Check it out. Marco did this one," he says, pulling up his shirt to show me the ink on his chest I had been admiring all day. *Not all those who wander are lost* is written on his ribs.

Without thinking, I reach out and run my fingertips across the lettering. His breath hitches and I pull away. "It's beautiful. You did this, Marco?"

"Hell yeah, I did. Every tattoo he has, I've done. He's done all mine too. See?" He flashes me his man boobs. We all laugh when Elise hits him.

"Put your damn clothes on." She looks around the

restaurant before winking at me. "Tattoos are like crack to skanks."

We laugh and dig in to the best pizza I've ever tasted. I moan when I take a bite. "Oh my God, I didn't know pizza could be so good." I open my eyes and they're all just staring at me like I've gone crazy. "What? I've never gone out for pizza. It's usually frozen pizza or day-old takeout."

They all laugh at that. Noah wipes a drop of sauce off my chin, smiling.

"So, what led you and your brother here?" Elise asks.

I freeze, not knowing what to say. "Um… I don't really know. We had nowhere else to go, so why not here?" I cringe, hating the sound of my own voice telling our sob story.

Everyone's faces are serious, but it's Noah who breaks the silence. "Aren't your parents looking for you?"

I dip my head, shaking it. "No, my mom's always been a train wreck. We got in a fight and she walked out on us. It's just me and Matty. He didn't want us to get split up in foster care, and we couldn't afford to pay the rent she owed, so we ran."

"Shit, I'm sorry, Lexi. We shouldn't be so nosy."

"It's okay, really. She was never a mom to me

anyway, always messed up. It's better here with Matty. I just don't know how the whole school thing will work with no parents. Matty's barely eighteen. Pretty sure they'll send me to foster care if they find out I'm living with him."

"It'll be okay. Don't worry about all that. It's summer. Just relax and have fun. Anyway, you don't have just your brother anymore. Now you have us." Elise states this like it's an obvious fact.

I smile at her, my newfound friend.

We each chip in to pay and head outside to say our goodbyes.

"Lexi, give me your phone. I'll put my number in, and then you can text me when you're bored and need rescuing." I hand my phone over to Elise. She types away frantically at it before handing it back. "Text me anytime, okay?"

I nod. "Okay." I shake my head as she loops her arm in mine, and we fall in line behind the guys.

"You barely know me. Why are you being so nice? You could wake up tomorrow and realize I'm a mess."

She laughs a full belly laugh and almost falls over, pulling me with her. "Oh shut up. I love you already, Lexi. I'm not letting you go. I'm going to be so annoying, you'll rue the day you ever played Marco Polo with me."

We both laugh and talk about music and movies until we arrive outside my apartment. I don't want to go up there alone.

"You guys can, um… come up if you want." I lead them upstairs and into our tiny apartment. "It's not much. It's usually just me here. Matty's never home." I feel so nervous having them here. The guys make themselves at home, and I offer them a soda from the fridge as they sit down on the couch.

"It's awesome, just needs some love. We can hit up some thrift stores and give it a little style," Elise says, wandering around before settling on Marco's lap, leaving me to sit on the couch beside Noah.

"Oh! I have an idea!" she exclaims after a moment, jumping up.

"Oh shit, we're in trouble," Noah mumbles. We all laugh.

"Shut it, Noah. No one asked you." She winks at him. "Let's play twenty questions. It's a perfect way to get to know each other."

The guys groan, but I smile and sit on the floor cross-legged with her.

"Favorite ice cream flavor?" Elise begins.

"Mint chocolate chip."

"Me too."

"Favorite actor?"

"Zac Efron," I answer with a smile, my eyes finding Noah's.

She busts out laughing, pushing my arm. "Yes! His tattoos are hot."

Our little game goes on for a while, and the guys, finding Matty's PS4, start playing some shooting game.

A FEW HOURS LATER, THE DOOR SWINGS OPEN AND Matty walks in, freezing immediately when he sees us. His eyes narrow at the guys, then at me. "What the fuck is this, Alexa? Who are these people?" He's clearly not happy.

Elise stands up, walking over to him. She's fearless. I love her.

"Hi! You must be Matty. I'm Elise, that is my little brother, Noah, and that handsome fella there is Marco." Her cheerful face meets his scowl while she points out the guys. "We met Lexi today and became fast friends."

Matty just stares at her, confusion painting his expression. Even he can't bring himself to be a jerk to Elise.

"Well, as great as it is to meet you guys at two in the morning, maybe you should call it a night. Alexa, you can't stand up Z tomorrow morning."

"Who's Z?" Noah asks.

"He's her trainer. What the fuck is it to you?" Matty interrogates, glaring in Noah's direction.

"Matthew!" I chastise him for being rude. He ignores me, of course.

"Trainer? What are you training for?" Noah asks.

Once again Matty answers before I can. "Kicking the ass of anyone who tries to take advantage of her, that's what."

"Matty, stop being an asshole," I say, glaring at him. I turn and smile at Noah. "I guess it is pretty late. Thanks for coming over, guys." I lead them to the door.

Elise hugs me. "I'll text you tomorrow, okay?"

"Definitely. Thanks for today."

"Nice to meet you, Matty," she calls over my shoulder. He grunts in response.

They all file out. Noah's hand grazes mine as he walks by and winks at me. "Good night, Lexi."

I close the door behind them and turn to face the grumpy asshat that is my big brother.

"You let strangers in our home."

"Oh please, we didn't do anything wrong."

He sighs, running his hand through his hair. "You're right. Sorry, Lex, it was just a shock. Next time text me or something so I'm prepared to walk into a full house. Fuck, I'm tired."

"I'll let you know what I'm doing next time. It was an awesome day though," I offer with the biggest smile.

He gives me one in return and hugs me. "It's good to see you smiling, kiddo."

He disappears into his room, and I do a quick tidy before collapsing in bed. I'm going to be exhausted tomorrow. I lie in bed with a huge smile on my face, thinking about today.

My phone buzzes on my nightstand with an incoming text.

Noah: Hi.

I smile and squeal into my pillow. Noah is texting me! Elise must have programmed his number in when she had my phone.

Me: Hi back :)

The world's most eloquent speaker I am not. Excited energy is zinging through my entire body. I press my face into my pillow and scream.

Noah: Did u have fun today?

Me: Yes! Elise was sweet to let me tag along.

Noah: You'll never get rid of her now. She's

always wanted a sister LOL. It was great spending the day with you.

Me: It was nice to spend it with you too.

Lord, what is wrong with me?

Relax, it's just a guy. Just be normal, for the love of all that's holy.

Noah: Nice? Ouch... Here I thought I was aloof and brooding.

Me: Fancy words for a tatted skater punk LOL... FYI you were in fact aloof and brooding.

Noah: So... your brother... he's intense.

Me: He is, yeah.

Noah: Does he let you date?

Me: Don't know, it's never come up.

My heart is racing. Is he really going to ask me out?

Noah: Do you think he would let you go on a date with me?

Me: I don't see how he could stop me ;)

Noah: Can you really kick my ass?

Me: Why? U planning to do something that requires an ass kicking?

Noah: Wouldn't dream of it, sweetheart. Any plans tomorrow?

Me: I'm supposed to go to Elise's after the gym.

Noah: Cool. Text me after your ass-kicking lessons :)

Me: Okay, I better get to sleep. Good night, Noah.

Noah: Sweet dreams, Lexi.

I LIE THERE STARING AT HIS TEXT. *SWEET DREAMS indeed.* This whole day was like a dream. I can't believe Elise and Marco are married and expecting at their age! You can tell she's going to be an amazing mother, and I get to watch it all. They're so sweet with each other. I couldn't imagine being married at eighteen, though it suits them just fine.

Seeing Noah again was… surreal. I'd be lying if I said I hadn't thought of him more than once since we first met. There's something calming about him that sets him apart from everyone else. I've had this huge wall up in my life between me and everyone really, especially the opposite sex. I never wanted them to look at me the way Noah does. Never thought I would want their attention, but he makes me feel alive just by smiling. And the way my body sizzles when he's near me or when we touch…. It's exciting and terrifying. And completely new territory for me.

I run my fingers over the ridges of cuts lining my forearm, the sight of them ruining my good mood. Why would he want me? He knows I'm already broken. Tears sting my eyes. Why would he pick trash like me when he could have anyone? They probably only let me tag along because I was so pathetic. I told Elise my sad life story and she couldn't say no.

Erica's voice comes rushing in fast and furious. *"Whore. Stupid, useless bitch."* In my weakest moments, she's always there to bring me to my lowest.

With tears streaming down my cheeks, I reach a shaky hand into my nightstand drawer, taking out a small safety pin. I open it, touching the tip with my finger. It's sharp enough to do what I need but not suspicious if Matty goes snooping in my drawers. Razor blades are too obvious and would raise alarms. I've learned to be careful in my self-destruction. Bracelets and long sleeves cover most of the damage, and honestly, most people don't notice or care.

I pull the sharp tip across my forearm, leaving one line of blood in its wake, then another. With each cut my anxiety eases and I can block out the hateful voice intent on breaking me. Closing the pin, I put it away for safekeeping. The aftermath of my moment of weakness stings. Three angry-looking cuts across my forearm. I run my fingers over the lines, smearing the blood across my pale skin. I don't know what calms me more, cutting myself or watching the wound bleed and heal. If only the rest of me healed so easily.

I fall asleep clutching my wounded arm to my chest, wishing I were a little less broken. Dreaming of an aloof and brooding Prince Charming who will kiss away the pain of the world and make me whole.

FIVE

After dragging myself out of bed, regretting staying up so late last night, I walk like a zombie into Z's. The gym is alive with activity as always; I don't think this place ever sleeps. When I walk into Z's office, he's on the phone, so I collapse into the chair opposite his desk. I lean my head back and close my eyes, slowly drifting off.

The phone slamming down snaps me awake.

"You look like crap."

"Gee thanks, Z. I'm tired as hell. I was going to stay home but didn't want another lecture from Matty about respect," I reply, rubbing my hand over my face. "So here I am, showing you my respect." I wave my hand around in a mock salute.

"I think I'd rather you not show up at all than

come unprepared. But since you're here, let's get to it," he says, standing up and walking out the door. I scramble after him.

After working out for a while, I get up the nerve to ask the question that's been bugging me for weeks. "Why did you agree to help me? I mean, I know you own this place, but why are *you* training me? It's not like there are any other girls here." I motion around the all-guy gym.

"Doesn't take a genius to figure out why Matt asked me to make sure you can hold your own in a fight. When you first came in here, I could feel the tension radiating off you just being around me. I could tell that someone had hurt you, and it was up to me to make sure you were strong enough next time." He holds up his padded hands, and I start firing punches into them.

"How did you meet Matty?" I ask before repeating the punching pattern again.

"None of your business, kid. He helped me out of a jam once. That's all you're getting. Enough fucking questions."

I smile. He's like a big growling bear, but he's a good man. We continue our usual workout in silence.

"You're a good man, Z. I hope you know that," I

tell him before I head to the showers to get cleaned up for my shift at the front desk.

"Nah, I'm not, kid. You just don't know any better."

It's funny how good men never think they're good and bad men never think they're evil. I know a bad man when I see him, and though he may look the part, I know Z has a good heart. He gives me this feeling of empowerment, this spark of hope that next time life throws me down, I'll stand up and fight back. The world needs more men like him.

I RUSH INTO THE APARTMENT, DROPPING MY STUFF BY the door. Digging my phone out, I see Elise has texted me her address. I do a little happy dance. *Yay, I have a friend.* I let her know I'm on my way, then shoot a text to Noah.

Me: Hey! Heading to Elise's now.

Noah: Cool, see u soon.

I stare at his response. Will he be there?

Me: Is Noah at your place?

Elise: He lives here, so yeah.

Me: !!!

Elise: LOL Get your cute butt over here.

Me: Leaving now.

Grabbing my shoulder bag, I shove my camera in, grabbing my keys as I hurry out the door. The prospect of seeing Noah puts a skip in my step and a flutter in my heart. The address she gave me is only a fifteen-minute walk away. I put my earbuds in and crank my favorite playlist. Any excuse to slip into my own world.

The sun is shining, and I'm feeling strong after my session with Z. Of course, the cuts hiding under my sleeve are a constant dull ache in my arm, reminding me that no matter how strong I feel, part of me will always be weak. Part of me will always need to hurt myself to calm the noise in my head.

A HAND GRABS MY RIGHT SHOULDER AND INSTINCT takes over. I reach out, grabbing the hand and pulling the pinky back, while in the same motion I strike my right elbow back to take out my attacker. My elbow connects with a thud at the exact moment I see Noah's face. He doubles over, holding his head.

Oh crap! What have I done?

I pull my earbuds out. "Oh shit! Noah! Oh my God, I'm so sorry!"

"Fuck, you weren't kidding. You really can kick my ass," he says, laughing and shaking his head.

I smile at him. "You really shouldn't sneak up on people."

"Sneak up? I was yelling your name." His smile is slightly crooked and so incredibly kissable.

"Sorry, I was still in the zone from the gym, I guess." I can't believe I assaulted the first guy I've ever liked.

"It's okay. No blood, no foul. Come on." His hand is warm and strong as it takes mine, leading me into the apartment building. Elise is in the kitchen and Marco is lounging on the couch with a game controller in his hand when we walk in.

"Hey, Lexi, you find us all right?" Marco asks.

"I did, yeah," I say, looking over at Noah. We both burst out laughing. Elise walks in carrying two coffees. She hands one to Marco and snuggles in next to him, smiling.

"Hey, Lexi. What's so funny?" she asks.

"Lexi kicked my ass for touching her on the street," he admits, barely holding in his laugh. I slap his shoulder.

"You grabbed me from behind! What did you expect me to do?"

"Definitely didn't expect to be elbowed in the face and nearly have my finger broken. Seriously though, I pity anyone who tries to mug you. That was badass," he says with a sweet smile. A blush blooms on my cheeks.

"For real? Oh man, I wouldn't tell people. That shit's embarrassing," Marco says, laughing.

"You try it, she'll fuck you up too!"

"Nope, I think one of us getting our ass kicked by a little girl is enough for one day." He smiles at me.

"Coffee?" Noah asks. I nod and he leads me to the kitchen. Their apartment is bright and colorful; I can see Elise in every aspect of this place. It's very lived in, unlike mine.

"How long have you all lived here?"

"Just over a year. The three of us have always been close. I don't have a single childhood memory that isn't wrapped up in those two," he says, staring fondly at Marco and Elise on the couch.

I smile up at him. He's so handsome, his eyes so full of light. He steps closer to me, and the air between us sizzles. He closes the gap and brushes his soft lips over mine. I gasp at the feeling it creates in my body. I lick my lips, but with him so close, my tongue touches his bottom lip. He loses whatever control he was maintaining and kisses me full on, cupping my face. It is the single most spectacular moment of my existence. I cling to his shirt as we continue to explore each other.

Eventually he pulls back and looks deep in my eyes. We're both breathless.

"Damn," I whisper, breathless.

"You okay?"

"Better than okay."

A slow smile creeps in and he kisses my forehead, my nose, and then my lips again.

I bet he's kissed a lot of girls, slept with a lot of girls. My stomach clenches at the thought; I'm in way over my head with him.

"Hey… what's wrong?" he asks.

"I've never done this. I'm not any good at any of this. I feel like a child."

"There is nothing to get wrong here. I like you… a lot. Do you like me?"

"A lot," I say, nodding and smiling.

"Well, then, the hard part's over." Taking my hand, he kisses the back of it before we settle into the living room with Marco and Elise and easy conversation.

After an hour or so, the guys announce they need to get to work, which is at Marco's uncle's tattoo parlor. They're newbies and must pay their dues before becoming artists themselves, whatever that means. They have these dreams of how they want their lives to work out. I always figured I'd either end up a junkie like Erica or dead. Never crossed my mind that I'd make it out of there alive, so to be honest, I've never given my future a second thought. But now I see a bright future stretching out before me with so many possibilities, so many dreams to be dreamt.

Elise and I spend the day wandering through the neighborhood shops, holding baby outfits against her tiny baby bump and debating baby names. I, of course, take as many pictures of her as possible.

Another perfect day.

THIS BECOMES THE NEW NORM FOR OUR GROUP. Either we're all at my apartment or theirs, just hanging out. Noah and I are taking it slow—epically slow. A few kisses here and there, some hand holding, but I know he's careful not to push me any further. And for now, I'm grateful. These three people have quickly become so important to me, and I'm terrified they will be taken away. Life has a way of kicking you just when you think everything is going to be all right.

·   ·   ·

MATTY IS GETTING BETTER. HE'S NICE TO ELISE whenever she's around, but he's still on edge when the guys are over. I know he worries about me, but I wish he'd see I'm not so weak anymore. He knows Noah and I are together but leaves us be for the most part. He knows sex isn't something I will ever rush into. Even after a month with Noah, I'm still not there yet.

ELISE AND I ARE SITTING IN THE PARK HAVING TEA. My sleeve slips up my arm, and when she catches a glimpse of the tiny scars lining my forearm, she gasps. After years of cutting, it's a railroad track of thin lines from the inside of my left elbow to my wrist. Most are quite faint and can't easily be seen, but a few are deeper and stand out in harsh red lines.

"What have you done to yourself?" she asks, grabbing my arm and pushing the sleeve up. I try to pull away, but she holds it firm. "Oh, Lexi, please say you aren't still doing this to yourself." She looks at me with tears in her eyes.

"It's not as bad as it looks. I've... I've gotten a lot better lately," I stammer, trying to reassure her.

"Why do you do it?"

"At first, I think I did it because I felt so angry

and helpless. Sometimes my head gets so loud I can't breathe. This quiets everything. It calms me when I can't get my mom out of my head."

"Don't give her power, Lexi. What you're doing to yourself, it gives her control over you. You need to stop. Please tell me you'll stop."

"I'm trying, Elise. I promise I am." It's the truth. I've only slipped once since Jax's house.

She pulls me into a hug. We're both wiping at our cheeks when Noah walks over.

"What's wrong?" He looks so concerned.

I shake my head, tugging on my sleeves.

"Nothing, just girl stuff," I reply, avoiding Elise's sad face.

She pats my arm and then my cheek before standing up. Her once little baby bump seems to have ballooned into a very large baby bump almost overnight, turning her walk into a bit of a waddle. She looks radiant pregnant. I take her picture constantly. She photographs beautifully; it's like her soul radiates through the lens. Her child is going to be so lucky to have a mom like her.

"Where are your thoughts running today?" Noah asks, tapping my nose.

Smiling up at him, I stand and wrap my arms around his waist, nuzzling into his chest.

"I was thinking what my life would have been like if I had a mother like Elise."

He kisses the top of my head and rubs my back. Not feeding me sweet empty words but comforting me nonetheless.

"Stay the night with me tomorrow?" he asks. My body goes rigid, I don't know what to say. He pulls me back, obviously seeing the panic in my eyes. "Hey, I'm not expecting anything to happen. I want to fall asleep next to you and wake up with you in my arms." He leans down and kisses me. I melt into him as I always do.

"Okay."

His eyes sparkle when he smiles. "Really?"

Looking unsure, I nod and smile. The thought of curling up in his arms sends a shiver over my body. One he notices.

"I know I'm irresistible. Try to keep it in your pants though."

I shake my head. "You're trouble, Noah King, sexy stranger in the dark."

"It's a good thing you love trouble, then," he says, dipping me into a kiss. I hold on for dear life at first, overwhelmed by this all-consuming feeling taking over me.

"I do, you know… love you," I admit, gazing into

his deep dark eyes. I've never said that to anyone before. I feel like I just handed him a knife and exposed my jugular.

He just stands there, not saying anything.

"Crap, I'm sorry. That was weird. I shouldn't have said that. It was a nice moment and I ruined it. Ignore me," I say, backpedaling, pulling his hands off me so he doesn't see me crying. I'm so stupid. Of course he doesn't love me. I'm such a fucking loser. I grab my camera, ramming it in my bag. I want to disappear, to run away before I break down completely.

"Stop. Lexi," he says, touching my shoulder, but I step away so his hand falls. I duck my head so he can't see my face.

"Whatever, it's fine. I get it. Matty's waiting on me." I shoulder my bag and turn my back to him as the tears start to fall.

"Jesus, Lexi, just fucking *stop*!" He grabs my shoulders, spinning me around. "Stop running away and look at me." He pulls at my chin, tipping my head enough that he can see I'm crying.

"Please… I'd rather you say nothing at all than tell me you don't love me. Just let me go." I clench my eyes shut for a moment, willing the tears to stop.

"I love you, Lexi. Of course I love you," he confesses, looking at me like I might break.

"You do?" I whisper.

He nods as he brushes my hair behind my ears. I laugh and a whole new batch of tears starts falling. He shakes his head and pulls me into a fierce hug. "I've never told anyone I loved them before. It's a big deal to me. I needed a minute to process."

I exhale a breath I didn't know I was holding and hug him tight at his reassurance.

AFTER DUMPING MY BAG INSIDE MY ROOM, I TEXT Matty saying I'm home and will be staying over at Elise's tomorrow night, which is not technically a lie. She's slept over at our place a few times; Matty likes her but hates that she calls him Matty like I do. It cracks me up watching his eyes roll, but he always smiles. I think it makes him happy that I have a friend.

I know the responsibility of taking care of me is stressful, and summer is almost over. The issue of registering for school and all the questions that will bring up is scaring us both. We have no idea what to do when the time comes. I have ID but no legal guardian. Matty is only eighteen; there is no way they'll let him be my guardian, and he probably wouldn't want the job, to be honest. What eighteen-year-old wants to raise his kid sister instead of being young and carefree? Though I don't ever remember seeing Matty carefree. He always looks like the weight of the world is on his shoulders. He's almost never home anymore. We text, but that's our only contact. When I see food has been eaten or the house is a little messier than I left it, those are my only clues he was home.

I asked what he's doing for money once and he flipped out, saying life is expensive and there are no right choices. Whatever that means. I assume he's stealing cars; it makes the most sense, and Noah agreed. He confessed that he's seen him hanging out with some pretty sketchy people. The kind of people who you do not want to cross.

I'M AWOKEN IN THE NIGHT BY A LOUD CRASH COMING from the kitchen. My whole body erupts in a cold sweat, but even though I'm terrified, I peek out my door to see what's happening. I spot Matty hunched over the sink, coughing. I flick the light on and almost faint from the sight of him. He's covered in blood. His eyebrow is split, as is his bottom lip, and his left eye is swollen shut. He's a mess.

"Oh my God! What happened!" I cry out, rushing over to him. I have no idea what to do. "Who did this to you?" I ask, pressing a towel against his eyebrow. My stomach lurches at the sight of his skin split open. He needs stitches. "You need to go to the hospital."

"I can't go to the hospital! Just fucking help, Alexa!" he yells at me, the booze on his breath so strong it makes me gag.

I try to get myself under control and focus on cleaning him up as best I can through the tears. If there's one thing we know how to do, it's to clean up after taking a beating.

"Please tell me what happened." I plead with him, but he pushes me away.

"You wouldn't understand. You sit here all happy in this new life, and that's great, Lexi. I'm glad things are better for you. You deserve to be happy. But for me, this place is no different than the last. Every day I'm backed into a corner. I'm fighting to survive, only now I've got to fight for both of us. You have no idea what it's like for me. What it costs me to live in this shithole."

"Matty, I had no idea. I can give you money, I could help if you'd just let me."

"You can't help! You don't even belong with me. You belong in foster care. I'm not supposed to be taking care of you. I'm fucking everything up!" He starts pacing, pulling on his hair. "I was supposed to be the one to take care of you, and I can't do it anymore." He's completely losing his cool.

I tear up; I can't stand hearing him say these things to me.

"Please don't leave me, Matty! I need you!" I reach out to grab his arm, and when he jerks out of my grasp, I break down crying. Anger floods me at his dismissal. "Why take me at all if you were just going to leave me like she did?"

"You think I had a fucking choice? I have no choices! I never have!" He's never screamed at me like this.

Running to my room, I slam the door behind me. I can't calm my breathing and sobbing. He hates me, wishes I wasn't here. With a shaky hand, I dig around in my drawer for something to carve the pain out of my life, to calm the chaos in my soul. The thin red line isn't enough this time, so I pull the pin across again and again and again, leaving frantic scratches all over my forearm until my heart calms and my breathing slows.

The guilt settles almost immediately. I survey the damage; I'm a fucking mess. I can't breathe in this apartment. I need to get out of here.

I grab my things and run out the door. I can't stay here. I can't watch another person I love leave me. He doesn't try to stop me. I run the whole way to Noah's, and I'm breathless when I arrive, banging on their door in the middle of the night.

Noah opens the door in his boxers, rubbing his messy bed hair. He takes one look at me and his eyes widen in shock. "What the fuck happened to you?" He pulls me inside, and I break down crying. He picks me up and sets me on the kitchen counter.

"Did he hit you?"

I look at him, confused, and then down at my hands. They're still stained in my brother's blood, and my sleeve is stuck to my forearm with dried blood.

"No! Matty came home beaten up bad. He won't tell me what happened or who did it, and he just lost it on me. Told me he was sick of taking care of me. That he didn't want to do it anymore," I say between sobs. "I don't know what happened. I snapped and couldn't stop cutting. I'm so sorry. I was doing better, I swear. I'm sorry." I'm so ashamed that he's seeing me like this, at my worst.

"It'll be okay, Lexi. You can stay here as long as you want." He kisses my forehead. My anxiety level is coming down, and I feel exhausted.

Noah leads me into the bathroom, turning on the shower and waiting as steam fills the room.

"Shower this blood off and I'll bring you something clean to wear to bed, okay?" he says gently.

I nod, taking off my blood-covered clothes and stepping under the soothing hot water. What am I going to do now? Matty hates me.

Long after the blood washes away, I continue standing under the water until it goes cold.

Noah's hand reaches in, turning the water off. He pulls me out of the shower and dries my body. I just stand there, staring at the floor, lost, not caring that I'm naked. He pulls a shirt over my head and shorts up my legs, rolling the top a few times so they fit. After inspecting my forearm with a stoic expression and furrowed brow, he sprays some antibacterial stuff on my cuts before wrapping my arm carefully. Then he pulls me toward his bedroom.

"You okay. Lexi?" Marco asks, peeking his head out of his room.

"Tomorrow, Marco. She needs sleep" is all Noah says to him before closing the door behind us.

He pulls me down onto the bed with him, and I rest my head on his chest, listening to his heart beating.

"Everything will be better tomorrow. Sleep. I'll keep you safe," he whispers.

I sigh, exhausted, and can't keep my eyes open any longer.

"I love you, Noah. I'm sorry."

"You have nothing to be sorry for, sweetheart. I love you too. Now sleep."

I curl into him as his heartbeat lulls me to sleep. Tomorrow will be a better day. Matty will apologize, and things will be better.

AFTER WAKING UP TO A TEXT FROM MATTY SAYING he's sorry, I decide not to go home today. Matty and I need a break from worrying about each other. I call Z and let him know I won't be in for a few days. He's been training a new girl for the job, and she's more than capable of taking over for me. School is around the corner, and it was only meant to last the summer anyway. I tell him I'll be in next week for our regular session.

We're all up early talking and laughing over coffee and making crazy plans for after I graduate. One year and I'll be free and old enough to make my own choices. Good or bad, my future will finally be in my own hands.

"I'd like to live near the beach. I've never seen the ocean," I say with a shy smile.

"Me either," Noah, Marco, and Elise all say at the same time, causing us to burst out laughing.

"This is the saddest thing ever! Four people born and raised in California, and not one of us has seen the ocean," Elise says, shaking her head.

"It's settled, then. Get up! We're going right now." Noah stands up, holding out his hand to me.

"Are you serious?" My eyes are wide as butterflies flutter in my stomach.

"Hell yeah, let's do it. It's what, a four-hour drive to the coast? What else are we going to do today? None of us have work. What do you say?"

"Yes! Oh my God, Noah, you are brilliant. Let's do it. I want to feel the ocean on my toes before this baby comes," Elise squeals excitedly.

We pick up some snacks and drinks while fueling up the Jeep, and drive west. I text Matty saying I'm sorry too and that I'm spending the day with the gang. He doesn't reply.

"Your brother okay?" Elise asks, seeing me texting.

"I hope so. He's not answering though. Maybe he's really hurt?" I regret running out on him when he needed me.

"I'm sure he's fine. Just take today for yourself, okay? No worrying, no stress, just a relaxing day at the beach." Noah kisses me, and I lean into him, watching the desert landscape pass by the window.

I must have fallen asleep at some point, because Noah's voice wakes me.

"We're here," he whispers, brushing his lips against my temple.

I smile up at him, and then my eyes go wide when I realize where we are. I jump up, nearly hitting his head.

"We're here?" I look out the front window, seeing Elise and Marco hand in hand walking barefoot in the sand. I clamber out, kicking off my shoes as I go, and let my toes slip into the warm sand. I close my eyes and relax into the bliss. Feeling a shadow over my face, I look up into the deep dark eyes of my love. I stand on my toes and wrap my arms around his neck, pushing my fingers into his hair.

"Thank you for this." I kiss him gently at first, but something in me comes alive and I pull his hair to bring him closer, deeper, wanting more. We break apart after several moments, breathing heavily.

"That was one hell of a thank-you. Come on," he says with a smile, pulling me toward the ocean.

It's everything I ever dreamed it would be: deep blue water, almost black, the waves crashing relentlessly against the shore. It's so powerful, my heart feels like it's about to burst. Tears fall on my cheeks and I recognize this as home, like the ocean is what has been missing from my soul.

I walk right in up to my knees until the first wave crashes into my legs, almost knocking me over. Noah stands behind me, arms wrapped around my waist, keeping me stable as wave after wave crashes around us. This is the best day of my life, right here and now with the people I love most.

"This is heaven on earth. I never want to leave," I say to myself.

Elise comes up beside me and loops an arm in mine. I lean into her and put a hand on her swollen belly. The four of us stand in the water, eyes on the horizon. Nothing can dampen our spirits on such a brilliant day.

"We'll bring your sweet baby girl here every day.

She'll learn to walk with her little toes curled in the sand. This is such a magical place. Nothing bad could ever happen to her here. She'll be safe and loved and protected," I say, crying. I wish so many magnificent things for them and their baby.

Elise is crying now too. "This is where we should live when you turn eighteen. We'll be a real family, all of us."

"You two are always crying," Marco says, shaking his head.

"Happy tears, my love. Happy tears from this day on." She wraps her arms around him.

I pull out my camera and snap a bunch of pictures. Seashells, our toes in the sand, everything I can to remember every detail. Elise then snatches my camera to take a few pictures of Noah and me. It is the single most amazing day of my life. I never want it to end.

We lie on a blanket in the sand and make crazy plans for where we'll live here and what we'll do with our lives. The guys plan to open their own tattoo shop. I'll be a photographer, shooting weddings and families. Elise declares she'll take care of us all, baking cookies and chocolate cakes and being the best mom ever.

Divine dreams of a flawless future.

By the time we drive back home, it's late, so I stay over. "A perfect end to a perfect day," Noah says against my ear while we're wrapped in each other's arms in his bed. His gentle heartbeat echoes my own in the darkness.

I turn to face him, getting lost in those dark eyes. I run my fingertips over his lips. My overpowering feelings for him scare me; they fill me with hope and love, make me feel worthy of both. Pressing my lips against his, I feel an overwhelming urge to do something crazy and brave.

Reaching down, I pull my shirt over my head in one swift movement before I chicken out. His gasp is barely audible. I pull him to me; the feel of his warm, hard chest against my naked body makes me moan. He answers with what sounds like a growl. He kisses me deeply, and I fall in love with him all over again in this moment.

"I love you, Lexi," he says, kissing me. And I believe him. I feel his love for me in everything he does. I never thought I would feel this way. An overwhelming contentment envelops me in the arms of this man I love.

I run my hands down his neck, over his tattooed chest, loving the freedom to explore his incredible body. He moves over me, settling between my legs, kissing his way down my neck. When his mouth explores my naked form, I can barely contain my moans. He continues worshiping me with his hands and mouth until I'm so worked up my whole body aches with craving. His hard length rocking against my core drags another moan out of me, and my hips move against him involuntarily, needing to feel more of him. My body is a live wire, teetering on the edge of something that's building inside, something I've never experienced. I reach out and wrap my hand around his length. His breath hisses out of him as he pushes himself against my hand. I revel in his body's reaction to my touch, the way I can make him feel.

"Do you have a condom?"

His eyes widen at my words. He reaches across his bed to his nightstand, pulling out what I asked for. "You sure about this?" His breath catches as he stares down at all of me, exposed and desperate for him.

I sit up, cupping his cheek. "I want you, all of you. I need you, Noah."

I watch with bated breath as he slides the condom over his considerable length.

Then he pushes into me, painfully slow, the full-ness stealing the breath from my lungs.

"Are you okay?" His body is rigid. I see worry

seeping into his eyes.

I smile, kissing his sweet lips. "Better than okay." I roll my hips, kissing him again; he groans and starts moving with me.

I dig my nails into his arms and drag them over his back, desperate to have him impossibly closer. Everything is so intense, every feeling, every touch simultaneously too much and not enough. We crash into each other with an unrelenting force that sweeps us away toward climax.

"I love you, Lexi. I know it's crazy, but I swear I'd marry you today," he confesses as we lie in bed clinging to one another.

I laugh into his chest, my hand on his heart. "You saved me when I thought the huge world was this dark, evil place. You showed me what love could be. I will love you for the rest of my life, Noah. I'd totally marry you, just FYI," I say, kissing him.

We lie there silent for a while before I ask, "Would you give me my first tattoo?"

He looks down at me, smiling. "Of course. Anything you want, angel," he whispers, kissing my shoulder.

We fall asleep in each other's arms as the sun starts to rise.

Best day ever.

SIX

Tattoo day is a go. It took a good hour of talking to decide which little words or pictures the guys could do easily here in the apartment. They have their own tattoo gun and are damn talented, if you ask me. Elise had a brilliant idea for a tattoo for me.

"I read that some people will draw butterflies on their friend's arm to make the cutter think of someone they love, who loves them, before they cut. Whenever you feel hopeless this will remind you that we love you, and you don't have to hurt yourself," she says. She won't be silent about my cutting; she thinks the more we talk about it, the less I'll want to do it.

I like the concept though. I look over at Noah,

who hates the idea of me hurting myself. There's a grim line on his face for a moment as he looks at my arm. He must like Elise's suggestion though, because he picks up his sketch pad and proceeds to effortlessly sketch out four beautiful delicate-looking butterflies that will cover the scars of my self-hatred and replace them with love.

"One butterfly for each of us who love you: Matt, Marco, Elise, and me," he says as I run my fingers over each delicate butterfly.

"Beautiful." Tears start running down my cheeks. I feel so overwhelmed.

"Don't cry, Lexi love." He brushes the tears from my cheeks and lays a perfect kiss on each eyelid.

"Happy tears," I reassure him, hugging him tight.

"That's awesome, Noah!" Elise peeks at his sketch. "I've gotta be at work in thirty minutes, so I better start waddling now."

"I'll take you, babe." Marco grabs his keys. He doesn't like to leave her alone anymore, and he constantly hovers. It's cute.

"Have fun. And you better make my butterfly the biggest and prettiest." She winks before she and Marco walk out the door.

"How much longer will she keep working?" I ask.

Noah shakes his head. "We keep telling her she

should quit, but she claims she's just fine waitressing until she's due. She's stubborn," He keeps doodling away on his sketch pad. It amazes me the things he can create.

He puts it down and claps his hands, smiling. "You ready for this? Depending on your pain threshold, this could hurt like a bitch." The timbre of his voice sends a shiver through my body.

"I'm ready."

He starts prepping the station, and I watch him go through the motions, admiring the way his muscles stretch and contract.

"Hop up, babe," he says, patting the chair.

I sit down and put my arm on the armrest. He preps my forearm and applies the stencil in just the right spot, avoiding the most recent cuts. He looks up at me. "Good?" he asks.

I nod, but the second the gun starts up, I jump.

He chuckles beside me. "Try not to do that. We don't want deformed butterflies."

With a wink, he starts to work. I watch it take shape with each pass of the gun, each dip in the ink, and I can't stop staring at his skill.

"Why did you start cutting?" His voice is quiet but strained. His eyes dance over the scars across my arms that he's trying to cover. "You don't have to answer that if you don't want to."

My stomach clenches with worry. I hate talking about it, but I know he won't judge me. "A few years ago. I think I was twelve. Erica was being awful, and Matty wasn't there to stop her, so I took a beating." The physical blows were never as hard as the words she threw at me like daggers. "Her words just sank in somehow, and now in my weakest moments, she's there, ready to remind me how useless I am, that my mother never wanted me. I try to ignore it, but sometimes it's so loud that it's all I hear."

"And that morning at Jax's? Did you really try to kill yourself?"

I groan and cover my face with the arm he isn't working on. "No, it was just a stupid, weak moment. I had never seen a razor blade before, and it was sharper than I expected. When Jax burst in the door, my hand slipped and it looked so much worse than it was. I don't want to make excuses, but I was feeling low and lost in the world. I fucked up. I haven't cut in a while, I swear. I'm doing much better."

"I don't want you to hurt yourself, Lexi. I can't take the thought of it. It kills me to know you felt so lost and alone. As long as I'm alive, you will never be alone."

He finishes the tattoo in comfortable silence. It's mesmerizing watching him, and before I know it he's sitting back, admiring his work.

"It's so beautiful. Thank you," I say, hopping off the chair and placing a quick kiss on his sweet lips.

"Didn't hurt too much, did it?" He sounds concerned.

"No. I mean, it wasn't fun, but it's worth it."

When Marco comes home from taking Elise to work, he leans over Noah's shoulder, checking out my tattoo before heading in the direction of the kitchen.

I can't stop staring at the tattoo before Noah goes about wrapping it up, giving me cleaning tips for the next few days, a speech I'm sure he's given a dozen times at work.

"I wish I could draw like you guys. Your work is art." I'm looking through a photo album they've started. There's only about twenty photos, but still their talent is clear.

"Of course it's art. But you could totally do it. Here, tattoo me," Marco says, holding out the tattoo gun.

I wave him away. "You're insane. I can't just tattoo you!" I'm shaking my head, but then I smile. "I couldn't… could I?" I look at Noah, then back at Marco. They're all smiles.

"Here, I'll make it easy for you." Marco gets up, grabs a pen off the table, and walks over to the mirror on the far wall. He writes something on his forehead above his left eyebrow, then walks back to sit in front of me. I burst out laughing. Above his eyebrow he wrote the word *ART,* but backward!

"You can't be serious! Marco, the letters are—"

I'm interrupted by Noah coughing. I look over at him; he's laughing and shaking his head at me, obviously wanting this to happen. "Do it, Lex, or I swear I will."

I pick up the gun, and since I spent the morning watching Noah do mine, I get a feel for it quickly. Noah comes to sit behind me, wrapping his arms around me, guiding my hand while I start immortalizing Marco's stupidity on his forehead.

"You are so going to regret this, dude," I say to Marco.

He just shakes his head. "No regrets, man."

I start to trace over the letters. Really it's Noah doing all the work; I'm just holding the gun. It only takes a few minutes and it's finished. Marco stands up and looks in the mirror at our handiwork, then smiles.

"That's wicked." He turns, looking at me all proud.

"Can we tell him yet?" I whisper to Noah, but he shakes his head.

"Nah, wait for Elise's reaction. It'll be way more fun this way." I can feel him shaking with laughter behind me.

"You are the worst best friend ever," I whisper in his ear.

"He'd do the same to me, babe. Believe me." He kisses me, and we fall back on the pillowed floor, making out.

"Dudes, for real? I'm right here!" Marco yells in mock outrage.

We come up for air, laughing at Marco's feigned disgust. A thought hits me out of the blue.

"Ooo!" I squeak excitedly, "I want the coordinates to the beach we went to tattooed on my right wrist."

"See, Noah, she's already addicted. But seriously, that's a great idea. I'm in. We should all get one," Marco suggests.

"They're pretty long though. Maybe we should break them up. Elise and I can get the latitude, and you guys can get the longitude. Like pieces of a puzzle."

"That's a cool idea. I like it." Noah kisses my new tattoo, now bandaged up.

And just like that, my addiction to ink begins. I know I'll want more; I can feel it in me already. I see now why people cover themselves in beautiful ink, writing their history on their skin, like a photo album you take everywhere you go. The adrenaline rush it gives me is intense, like I could take on the world.

"I've got the afternoon shift at Z's. Then I'll run home. Matty still hasn't answered any of my texts," I say, standing up.

"I have to be at work in an hour, but I can walk you," Noah offers.

"Aw, escorted to work by a sexy guy? Yes please. Though I'm dreading seeing Matty afterward."

"I can come with you later if it'll make you feel better."

"No, but thank you for offering. We need to have it out, and I think if the sexy guy sleeping with his baby sister is in the room, it would only piss him off. But I'll allow you to walk me to work," I say, running

my hands up his arms and around hi
him down for a kiss.

"Sexy guy. I got an upgrade from sexy
huh?" His arms surround me, hands cupping
butt. I moan, pressing into him.

"Guys! Come on, you're going to make me go
blind," Marco yells, covering his eyes.

We both laugh, and I grab my bag on our
way out.

Dreading my showdown with Matty, I'm glad for
my shift at Z's gym. We stopped our training
sessions a week ago. Now I have free rein to come
work out whenever I feel like it. Sad to say it's been a
week since I stopped in.

The new receptionist is on the phone as I come
in the door. I kiss Noah goodbye before he leaves.
She smiles and wiggles her eyebrows, pointing to
Noah's back. She's hilarious, and I wish we had shifts
together instead of opposites.

She's doing a way better job than I ever could, but
I miss being part of the gym on a steadier basis now
that I'm down to one shift a week. Summer is wrapping up, and the school issue I've been ignoring will
need to be figured out. Maybe Z could adopt me.

Z appears out of nowhere. "Long time no see.

know, you can come around even on days you
don't have to work. Or are you too cool to work out
now that you have a man?"

"What do you know about me having a man? You
listening to gossip now, Z?"

"People say things. I listen." He shrugs. "He a
good guy?"

I can't help but smile at this. "Yeah, he's a great
guy."

"Well, I suppose you know how to kick his ass
now if he wasn't."

I start laughing, remembering how I did in fact
kick his ass. "I totally did. I was walking, completely
zoned out. He put his hand on my shoulder to get
my attention because I had my earbuds in, and I
went full attack mode on him."

Z's rough, throaty laugh comes out in a burst so
loud that everyone in the gym stops and looks at
him. His laugh is infectious. "That's fantastic, kid."

The rest of my shift goes on as usual, answering
phones and filing paperwork. But the time alone
allows my impending confrontation with Matty to
stir in my head until my stomach swirls with
anxiety.

Once my shift is over, I head home and unlock
the door. The apartment is quiet inside; he's not

home. Why am I surprised by that? He's never home.

With a sigh, I walk into the kitchen, grabbing a bottle of water out of the fridge. How is this fight ever going to end if he won't talk to me? I shoot him a text, letting him know I'm home and to please come see me.

My heart sinks when I see the bloody towel from the other night still in the sink. As I walk down the hall, I see a fist-size hole punched through his bedroom door. "Oh, Matty, what did you do?" I peek in his messy room, but it's empty. I hate being here alone. I grab some clothes and shove them in my bag with shaky hands. I don't like leaving like this, but I would rather stay with Elise and Noah than be here alone.

I leave a note on the counter in the kitchen, letting him know I'll be staying at Elise's until he calls or texts me, but I've got a sick feeling in my stomach about leaving, not knowing where he is and if he's okay.

———

"HE TRASHED YOUR APARTMENT?" NOAH ASKS ONCE I return to his place.

"It wasn't trashed, but he punched a hole in his door and threw some stuff around. He must have been so mad when I left." I should have stayed with him.

"It's not your fault he flipped out," he says, hugging me. "Just don't go back there alone, okay? I've heard some of the things he's been into, and if he's in as deep as they say, that's not a safe place for you."

I nod, holding on to him. "Matty wouldn't put me in danger. I'm sure everything's fine. I just wish he'd call me."

A WEEK GOES BY WITH NO WORD FROM MATTY. I'M sick with worry, and I can't seem to turn off my mind. It keeps racing through all the things that could have happened to him—or worse, he could have washed his hands of me and run away from the hassle of raising his kid sister.

"What do you mean, you're going back?" Elise asks from her comfy position on the couch. I can't see her face over her large belly.

"I forgot my laptop. It has every picture I've ever taken on it. I can't just leave it there. And I need to see if Matty left a note or something, see if he's been back or if he's…." I trail off, not wanting to admit that he might have left me. "I need answers, Elise. I won't be long."

"Noah's going to flip out! They'll be off work in another hour, and he specifically asked you not to go back there without them. Why don't we wait until they can come with you?"

"No, I'm just running over quickly to grab my computer and leave Matty a note. It'll take five minutes, tops," I say, standing and grabbing my bag.

She rocks herself back and forth a couple times, getting momentum to stand, insisting on coming with me.

"Stay here, Elise. I'll be right back," I say, but she's shaking her head.

"Nope, I'm coming with you and that's final. Let's go." She walks out ahead of me, standing outside the door with her arms crossed impatiently over her swollen belly.

I mumble something about her being a stubborn ass, but she just giggles and keeps waddling.

When we arrive at my apartment, we both freeze in shock. The whole place has been destroyed, and the door, which has an eviction notice stuck to it, has been kicked in and now hangs crooked on its hinges. Dread blooms in my stomach.

I take a step toward the door, but Elise grabs my elbow. "We should call the cops. Don't go in there."

Resting my hand on hers, I give it a squeeze, hoping to reassure her, but I don't feel any better about this situation. "Stay out here," I say, stepping into the chaos.

The couch is ripped up and flipped over. Anything that can break is broken. My heart is pounding in my chest. Who did this?

"Matty?" I call out, afraid to be too loud in case whoever trashed the apartment is still here. I step over broken glass and start toward my bedroom. Matty's room is destroyed, and there is blood smeared on his door and more spotting the floor.

Panic rises in my chest. I need to get out of here. I rush to my room; the door is open, and my stuff is thrown all over the place. Thank God I had my camera with me.

But my laptop is trashed. It looks like it was thrown against the wall.

"Lexi? I texted the guys. They're pissed like I told you and— Holy shit! What happened?"

I jump at Elise's voice in the other room. I toss the last few things I can fit in my bag and walk out to her. "I don't know. It was like this when I got here. He's not here. There's… there's blood all over his room," I say, tears falling down my cheeks.

"Maybe he just got in another fight. Come on, let's just go. You can text him from my place. We're not staying here. Let's go."

I don't know what else to do, how else to find him. I let her pull me toward the door—which is now blocked by two very scary-looking men.

I slowly maneuver myself between the men and Elise. "When you see an opening, don't hesitate. Run and get help," I whisper over my shoulder to her.

"I'm not leaving you!" she hisses, looking at the men with pure terror in her eyes.

"I can fight them, Elise. I know what I'm doing, but please, you have to run," I beg her.

She ducks her head but nods.

I look back at the men who are now stalking toward us into the apartment, predatory smiles painting their faces.

I decide to play the tough card. "Who the hell are you? Did you trash my apartment?" I point at the destruction. "Where's Matty?" I ask, suddenly regretting mouthing off to these scary guys. They position themselves for attack, and I shift toward the living room so I can get them away from the door, anything to give Elise a chance to run.

"We had to teach him a lesson. He stole from the wrong person this time. Now where's the fucking money?" he grumbles, pulling a gun from the back of his pants.

"Look, I don't know what you're talking about. You should leave now before the cops get here," I lie, trying to fake bravery.

They don't fall for it.

"You didn't call the cops, and we sure as fuck aren't leaving, not without our money."

There's no way out of this situation without a fight. I calm my breathing like Z taught me and stand with my fists up, ready to fight. It's obvious from the look on their faces that they think me fighting them is hilarious, and they both have a good laugh at my expense. Exactly the distraction I need. Asshats.

I punch the first guy in his nose, breaking it with a satisfying crunch, and swing a chair from behind me into his face. Then I swing my leg around connecting with asshole number two, knocking the gun out of his hand. When they're both down, I grab Elise's hand and we run for the door.

One of them grabs my ankle and I'm down. His

other hand quickly closes around my throat, cutting off my air.

Elise stands at the door, shaking, staring at me, crying. I shake my head at her, trying to tell her to run, but the words don't come out. My vision is going black, and the blows I'm hitting him with are doing nothing.

A gunshot rings out and the man holding me drops, allowing me to roll to the side, gasping for air. Elise stands behind the man who was choking me, a gun shaking in her grasp.

She shot him.

Oh my God, she *shot* him.

The gun clangs to the floor and she collapses, sobbing and clutching her round belly.

I run to her, falling on my knees. "Are you okay? The baby?" I ask, holding a hand on her belly. Her stomach jerks against my hand, startling me. Elise starts rocking back and forth, crying. I cradle her head to my chest. "It'll be okay. We need to go, Elise. We can't stay here," I tell her softly. I need her to move. We need to leave. Now.

"I killed him. I killed him," she keeps repeating.

I lift her chin, looking her in the eyes. I wipe away her tears and brush my hands over her hair.

"He was going to kill us. If you didn't shoot him,

we would both be dead right now. Do you understand? You saved us. Now please stand up. Let's go," I beg.

She nods, letting me help her to her feet. We make our way out of the apartment.

At the top of the stairs, loud noises ring out behind me. I'm thrown into the air as pain erupts throughout my body. My knees give out and I fall down the remaining stairs, cracking my head against the sidewalk. I lie there on the pavement, looking up at the sky as my vision begins to blur, incapable of moving as the life drains out of my body.

This is real.

I've been shot.

Something cold touches my hand and I look over. Elise is lying next to me, a line of blood running out of the corner of her mouth. Her eyes are locked onto mine, round with pure fear. One bloody hand is shaking and clutching at me desperately. The other is cradling her round belly.

"Elise," I cry, crawling closer to her, pain radiating through me. Blood has completely soaked the front of her shirt, coming from a hole in the left side of her chest. She tries to talk but chokes as blood spills out of her mouth. The whole world narrows as a black cloud encroaches my vision.

I try to press my hands on her wound, but my right arm isn't working. I ignore the pain shooting through me as my hands start shaking and my head spins wildly. I can't see her; something is in my eyes. I try to wipe it away, but the blood soaking my hands makes it worse. Falling onto the ground beside her, I clutch her hand as the life slowly drains out of us.

"I'm sorry."

We lie there taking our last breaths together.

Then Noah's voice comes from somewhere in the darkness.

Warm hands touch my face. It feels so real. I think I feel his lips kiss my palm, but his voice fades away like a leaf on the wind. I can't keep my eyes open. It's so cold.

In the distance, sirens approach.

Too late, I think before I let the darkness take me.

SEVEN

I WAKE TO A SLOW AND STEADY BEEPING. PAIN radiates over my whole body, and my head is pounding. It takes me a few tries to open my eyes, but when I look around the impossibly bright white room, it registers: I'm in a hospital room. Sensors are attached all over my body, and an IV is stabbed in my arm. As the events that led me here come rushing back, I start to panic, pulling at the wires with my right hand. I can't breathe. The beeping gets faster.

A nurse runs into the room, looking sweet and stern the way nurses do. "Stop tugging at those. You need to calm down, miss, though it's nice to see you're finally awake." After checking my IV, she picks up my chart and walks to the machine at my right. She writes something down and reattaches the sensors I managed to wriggle free while I stare at her in silence.

"Where am I?" I croak. My throat feels like it's on fire.

"In the hospital, of course." She states it like *Isn't that obvious?*

I shake my head and run my hand over the bandage on my left leg, cringing with the pain the movement causes in my right shoulder, which is also bandaged.

"You were shot twice. You've been out for a few days," she says.

I jerk up in bed. She can't be serious. "Days! What about Elise? Is she okay? I need to go. I need to see her."

"Whoa, whoa, settle down! You're not going anywhere," she says, trying to hold me down.

"Where is she? Is she on this floor? Can I see her? Just for a minute. I need to see she's okay. Did someone call my brother?" I blurt in a panic.

"Calm down, miss. I don't know who you're talking about. I'll go get the doctor to come check on you. Then, when you're ready, there's a police officer wanting to talk to you. He might have some of the information you're looking for. Just calm down before I'm forced to sedate you," she warns sternly.

I give up struggling and wait for more information. The doctor comes first, ignoring all my questions.

"Young lady, you are lucky to be alive. You were brought in with two gunshot wounds, one in the shoulder and one in the thigh. You've also suffered a concussion…."

I stop listening to him. The last thing I remember is holding Elise's hand. I need to know if she's okay. I need to see Noah. I need answers.

"The girl they brought in with me. Please, Doctor, she's my best friend. Can you tell me where she is? I just need to make sure she's okay."

He won't look me in the eyes. Once he finishes checking my wounds, he walks out without another word.

A few minutes later, a police officer walks in. He stands at the foot of my bed.

"I'm Officer Stevens. I was first officer on scene the night you were shot. You and another patient were being loaded into the ambulance when I arrived. One man was found dead in the apartment and one was shot in pursuit. It's your turn to answer a few questions. Could you tell me what you remember from that night?"

I nod, wanting to get this over with. "I went home to see my brother. The place was trashed and when we—Elise and I—tried to leave, two men were waiting at the door. We fought. One grabbed me by the throat, and Elise shot him. She only did it to save me. You can't charge her for murder when it was self-defense, can you?" I ask, my eyes filling with tears.

"No charges have been laid yet," he assures me while continuing to write notes. "Did you know the men? Had you seen them before? Were they friends of your brother, Matthew?"

"I didn't know them, no. But I doubt they were his friends. They kept asking me where the money was."

"What money?" he asks, his interest obviously piqued.

"That's what I said. I didn't know what they were talking about, but they made it clear they wouldn't leave without it. That's when they jumped me."

"And you fought them on your own. Two grown men," he asks skeptically.

"I tried to buy Elise some time to get away," I say, remembering how she didn't run like I told her to. I hope she's all right. She must be so scared. "Okay, I've answered your questions, now please answer mine. Where is Elise? I need to see her. Did anyone call Marco and Noah? Did you find my brother?"

He shakes his head. "We haven't found your brother, no. We have a Noah King and Marco Heart in custody. They were found on scene covered in blood when officers arrived. We've detained them until we got some answers."

"Elise must have told you they didn't do anything. They weren't even there when Elise shot the man. You have to let them go!" I say, getting frustrated that Noah was locked up for days while I lay here unconscious.

The officer shifts his feet and clears his throat. "They will be released shortly now that you have confirmed their story. I'm sorry, Miss Young, but the other gunshot victim was pronounced dead on arrival. You were the only survivor."

Only survivor.

The whole world drops out from under me.

"No! You're wrong. The girl who was with me, her name is Elise Heart. She's pregnant. She can't be dead!" I'm struggling with the lines attached to my body as I try to get out of bed. "She's not dead. I'll find her. She'll be okay. You're lying. She's okay. She's alive."

I start screaming, pulling at sensors attached to me and ripping the needle from my arm. The officer tries to hold me down, but I refuse to be stopped. I hit him and scream until more doctors and nurses come running in. Something jabs into my arm, and suddenly my limbs feel too heavy to move.

"She's not dead. She saved me. She has to be okay. She saved me. She can't be… she can't be…," I chant to myself, falling back on the bed and shaking my head.

She can't be dead.

I slip into unconsciousness and dream of Elise holding her baby on the beach at sunset. She can't be dead. God would never let something like this happen. I grasp onto the hope that I'll wake up and see her smiling face. This is all just a bad dream, a horrible mistake.

But it isn't a mistake. Elise is dead.

Through a cloud of sedation, they tell me no one has been able to find my parents and I'll be sent into foster care once I'm cleared for release. They tell me the girl who was brought in with me died on the street from a gunshot wound to her heart—her beautiful heart.

I sink into this fresh hell and refuse to hear any more. I scream and rock myself until the meds kick in.

I should never have gone back there. She asked me not to, but I wouldn't listen. This is my fault. I'm responsible for the death of my best friend and her unborn child.

I curl away from the words that hurt worse than the hole in my chest, words spoken with cold indifference by a doctor while I'm strapped down to a bed in the hospital.

My scars and outburst deem me a suicide risk. They keep me sedated until my body is healed enough that I can't cause damage to my wounds. I don't care anymore. I've got nothing left in me; I'm already dead. Like my mother, I'll happily keep myself drugged enough to not feel the pain of the world.

AFTER THREE WEEKS RECOVERING IN THE HOSPITAL, I slip up. Everything was closing in on me, and I couldn't breathe. In one moment of weakness while getting my bandages changed, I grabbed the scissors and tried to cut at my wrist. I swear I wasn't going to end my life. I just needed a quick release, a moment where I could breathe without pain. An orderly with a hero complex tackled me to the floor and disarmed me before I could cause any damage. My "suicide attempt" garnered me an extended stay in the psych ward for evaluation. In hindsight, I know it was a stupid move. Up until then, they saw me as a victim of a crime, not a mental case ready to end her life. But not anymore.

My circumstances—the fact that I'm an underage and homeless suicide risk—give the powers that be little choice other than placing me here at the "hospital" until I'm fully healed and finished with my therapy, both physical and mental. I don't care about getting better; all I can do is float along in this mind-numbing existence. Sleep, medicate, eat, therapy, sleep, medicate, eat, therapy. Lather, rinse, repeat until each pointless day blurs into the next.

No one comes for me. No one visits. Matty has gone missing, and Noah probably hates me for killing his sister. Why can't they just let me die? It's torture to keep on living this life when I stole Elise's from her.

THE GUNSHOT WOUNDS TO MY SHOULDER AND LEG are almost completely healed. It's been three months since the shooting with no word from my mother, brother, or Noah. I've officially been thrown away. Again.

I'm constantly being dragged from one therapy to the next: *"tell us about your childhood," "tell us why you're sad," "tell us why you won't speak," "tell us where the bad man touched you."* I've checked out mentally, so I can't answer their questions. I still don't understand how my life could change so drastically in a heartbeat.

Elise is dead. I swear I can feel her absence in the world.

Noah left me, taking all the light in the world and my sanity with him.

Matty and my own mother abandoned me.

I've never felt so alone.

It should have been me. Elise should be out in the world with her baby, living their happy life, and I should be cold in the ground.

I push food around my plate, unable to eat, and I don't sleep unless sedated. I stay up at night, going over every second of that day. Trying to work it out like a puzzle, wishing there was some way I could go back and fix everything.

I'm an empty shell. All the rejection and lack of love I carry with me from childhood comes rushing back. My mind screams horrible things at me: *I'm disgusting, unlovable. Noah left me. A waste of space that no one could ever love. I killed Elise and her baby. It's all my fault.*

I collapse from the weight of the words that have pierced my heart. Some days, I pretend to be over it, to be able to walk away from the pain of my childhood and the pain of being cast aside again, but the reality that Elise is gone, that Matty and Noah don't want me, is too much to bear. I'm desperate to make the pain go away, to try and cut it out of my body forever, but no matter how deep I cut, it stays. Useless, unloved, unwanted. Matty was my savior, the person who said he would take care of me. Noah promised he would love me forever. In the end, no one wants me. Everyone leaves. Pain is the only thing that stays, the only thing that's real.

My own parents didn't love me. Why should anyone else?

My eyes dance around the doctor's office, looking for something, anything to dull this pain, to quiet the voices telling me how little love I deserve. A set of keys sits on the desk in front of me; I imagine the sensation of pushing the little spikes into my skin and dragging. *Not sharp enough*. I pick them up, remembering the feeling of cutting. I hold the keys in a tight grip over my arm, willing myself to press down, but the butterflies etched into my skin remind me of the love I had once: the way Noah made me feel, the way being a part of a family made me feel.

I throw the keys across the room and cover my face, screaming. Breaking down completely. I've been thrown away by everyone who was supposed to love me. I feel the vomit rise in my throat as I run for the bathroom, unable to stomach how close I came to ending it all.

"BUT YOU DIDN'T CUT, ALEXA. THAT'S THE WHOLE point. You had the opportunity and chance, and you fought those urges. This is a good thing, small steps. You're taking each day, each episode as it comes. It shows great progress on your part. I think you're ready to leave this place," Roxanne, my caseworker, states in our therapy session. Like me almost slicing my wrists open is normal. Hell, for her it might be.

"I can't leave! What about Matty? No one has found him. Where would I go?" I ask, desperate for this one ray of hope.

"Alexa, I'm sorry, but there's been no trace of him. And unfortunately, your mother has an arrest warrant in Las Vegas, and with her track record, it's unlikely we'll find her. Even if we do, she'll be sent to jail. We'll be placing you in a foster care group home until we can find a more permanent placement for you."

I just stare at her, absorbing her words.

That's it. They've given up on me too.

"I don't care about Erica. Matthew is the only family I have left!"

"I assure you the police have been looking for him. If and when they find him, we'll notify you, but until then, this is what must happen. You will be placed in a group home, and you will attend school and start living your life. You can't simply press Pause on your life until he's found." She sighs. "Look, this isn't an ideal situation. I think it's time you accept that Matthew might not want to be found. Even if he's found, no judge would give custody to a barely legal sibling who is wanted for questioning over a murder case and the shooting of two innocent people."

"It wasn't his fault!" I know that's a lie. I know that whatever Matty was mixed up in brought those guys to our front door, but I know in my heart and soul he would never have intentionally put me in harm's way. I can't imagine the guilt he must be feeling over what happened that night.

I have no intention of sitting at some group home when I could be out looking for my brother, but I won't get the freedom unless I play along. So I nod. "Okay."

After packing my meager belongings in a lovely trash bag provided by my case worker, I say goodbye to one prison in exchange for another.

THE GROUP HOME IS EXACTLY AS I THOUGHT IT WOULD be: a cold, dark brick building where hopes and dreams go to die. I now live with a collection of broken, angry kids all intent on acting like prison inmates. Which is easy to do considering the ten-foot fence surrounding the property. This isn't a place where children go to be healed; this is a prison training center, grooming us to find our place in the underbelly of the unknown and unwanted. I need to get out of here as soon as possible before I too slip through the cracks.

Matty was right all along. He knew this was where I would end up if they found us.

I'm granted phone privileges after a week of good behavior. I can barely still my shaking hand as I frantically dial Noah's phone number, and with each ring my heart races. *Please pick up. Please pick up.*

"Who is this," a woman's clipped voice demands, and my heart stops dead.

"May I speak with Noah, please?" I ask politely.

"I repeat, *who is this?*" the cold voice demands once more.

"Uh, my name is Alexa. I'm a friend of Noah's."

Her gasp is audible through the line. "This is all your fault! He'll never speak to you again as long as there is life in my body. He hates you. It's your fault Elise is dead! It should have been you, you piece of trash. Don't ever call here again or I'll call the police!" She hangs up.

I stand there for a few moments in shock. He hates me. He thinks it's my fault. I collapse on the floor, still clutching the phone. He won't even speak to me. I mean, of course he won't talk to me. I killed his sister. I ruined his family's life, and the life of Elise's unborn child.

"I'm sorry," I whisper, dissolving into a pool of tears. Eventually I'm escorted back to my room where I curl into bed and wait for the world to end. Surely it can't keep going on like this. I can't keep breathing after everything has been ripped away from me. I let myself be stupid enough to believe life could be good. For a moment, I was deliriously happy. I gave love and was loved. It felt like a split second of time, like a dream. Only to wake up to this nightmare. Not only has it all been taken away, but it's my own fault. I destroyed a family with my stupidity. Why didn't I listen to Elise?

If only I could go back, stop myself from going. Stop everything from happening. The aching void in my heart begs the universe to please make it stop. This can't be real.

I rock myself in bed, willing time to rewind, willing Elise alive, willing Noah to love me again, willing Matty to find me and take me away from here.

I walk through the next week in a fog. I go to group therapy as required, I sit through classes as required, but I see and hear nothing. This is not where I'm supposed to be.

I WAITED EXACTLY ONE MONTH BEFORE MY FIRST escape attempt. I had no plan, no idea of how I would do it. I saw an opening and took it blindly.

The gate was open not fifty feet from me. I figured if I could make it out, I could find Matty, make Noah listen to me. Without thinking, I broke into a run, leaving that awful place in my dust. Closer and closer to freedom, I ran as fast as my legs would carry me.

I didn't even make it to the parking lot before they caught me. Flailing wildly, I was tackled to the ground and carried back inside, then locked in my room with the help of whatever sedative they stabbed into my arm.

"Son of a bitch." I cursed the hands that held me. I vowed to get out of there and find my brother. Nothing would stop me.

The second time, I thought I had planned everything to perfection. I watched the gate, watched the guards. I snuck out quietly and unseen, or so I thought. I stole some cash from another kid in my room and booked it out of there. They caught up to me at the bus station. Apparently, I'm not very original, and that was always the first place they looked for runaways. I went back without a fight this time.

For my third attempt, I spent weeks googling maps and found out we were only about a thirty-minute drive away from where I lived with Matty. I just needed to make it to the road, and then I could hitch a ride as far from here as I could get. No more buses, no more group home. I would find Matty myself.

I manage to actually make it out this time and am walking down the highway with my thumb out, begging for a ride, when a car of college girls picks me up. They're heading to a party and are happy to give me a ride home when I tell them my car broke down. As luck would have it, they drop me off right at my old apartment. I say my goodbyes and stand on the sidewalk, unable to stop staring at the spot on the pavement where I thought I was going to die, where I watched the life drain out of my best friend.

Thick tears fall down my cheeks as I stare at the stain in the cement. I sit there for I don't know how long. People shuffle past me; no one cares that my world ended in this very spot. They tread over the stains of our blood like it's nothing.

"I'm sorry, Elise. I should have listened to you. Please forgive me."

Eventually I pull myself away and tread up the stairs to our apartment, hoping by some miracle Matty will have left something, anything to tell me where I can find him.

Finding the door unlocked, I open it, hoping someone else hasn't moved in our absence. The apartment's spotless; any trace of the violence that occurred has been washed away. Makes me wonder how many people rent apartments after murders, having no idea the horror that occurred in their new home. All the rooms have been emptied out. All hope is lost.

I collapse on the couch and cry for the loss of my brother, feeling like there is nothing left anchoring me here.

"Alexa, you can't be here," Roxanne says from the doorway.

I start sobbing uncontrollably. I have nowhere left to run. "Where am I supposed to go?"

"You've got to stop chasing the past. Look forward, Alexa. You need to make a clean break. Your obsession with finding Matthew and loving this boy is ruining your progress and causing you to fall apart."

"I can't live without them. It hurts too much."

"I know this is hard," she says, wrapping her arm around me, "but you need to find a way to move on from this. I promise you, if I hear anything about your brother, I'll tell you."

EIGHT

AFTER BEING CAUGHT RUNNING AWAY THREE TIMES, I'm transferred to a foster home. We drive for hours. Obviously they think if they take me far enough away I won't try to escape. With each passing mile, the happy life I shared with my friends slips further away, and the hope of ever finding my brother disappears. I steady myself as we wind through the streets of a strange city and park in front of a small cottage. The house is decorated in suns, moons, and more wind chimes than I've ever seen in my life, like someone threw up an entire hippie commune all over the exterior of this poor little house. I look over at my case worker with wide eyes, questioning her choice. What fresh hell is this?

"You can't be serious," I say, pointing to the house.

"You only have one year until you age out of the system, Alexa. Lana Raine is her name, and she…, she's Erica's sister."

"My aunt?" I question, looking up at the house, trying to picture how this hippie fits in with Erica and her cruelty. "I didn't know she had a sister."

"It took some time finding her. But family is always preferable in these situations."

"If she's anything like Erica…."

"She's not. She has another foster child she adopted a few years ago. She may seem a bit… eccentric, but she's a good person, Alexa," she assures me.

I nod and look back up at the tacky house.

We walk up the cobblestone pathway to the porch. Every spare inch of the small space is decorated with pots of overflowing plants. Each pot is adorned with some mystical little creature, fairies and gnomes and little stones with sayings on them. It's cluttered but somehow seems magical and endearing. Whoever this woman is, it's obvious she is the polar opposite of the cynical Erica Young.

A sign hangs over the door: *Let your inner goddess shine.* I look back at my caseworker, pointing to the sign with wide eyes, shaking my head. She just smiles, shrugs, and rings the bell, not a doorbell but an *actual* bell attached to the wall beside the door. Who even does that?

Lana Raine appears in all her glory, like a vision in rainbow paisley. She looks like a bohemian princess with her wavy pale blonde hair hanging loose around her shoulders. Her colorful sundress flows straight down to her ringed toes. She leads us into her cozy home and I follow slowly, taking in the decor. I sit silently while Lana and Roxanne discuss my history and my recovery. I listen to my life spouted off like a stranger. I sound like a mess: broken home, gunshot victim, runaway. How is this my life?

She's Erica's sister, and for all I know, this could be a clever rouse—she could really be an ax murderer. I look around the room for any obvious signs of insanity and come up with nothing. Well, maybe she doesn't have the profile of an ax murderer, but sacrificing me to the Goddess in exchange for eternal beauty could be in her agenda.

Roxanne stands to leave and my heart lurches. *This is it. She's leaving me here.* She looks pointedly at me. "Be good, Alexa," she says before walking out, leaving me with Lana and her inner goddess.

"Are you hungry, sweetie?" she asks. I shake my head. "Come on, then, I'll show you to your room. You probably need a moment alone to process all of this." She stands and leads me up the stairs, stopping in front of a closed door. "This is my daughter Rebekah's room. She's your age and will be home for supper, so you can meet her then," she says, moving on. "This is your room, Alexa. You and Rebekah will share an adjoining bathroom." We walk into a very pretty room, and she points to a door on the far wall where I assume the bathroom lies. "I wanted to decorate, but your file mentioned you were an artist type, so I thought you'd like to put your own touches on the space. I've always loved this room. It has a great energy and light, don't you think?" She looks around, smiling.

Having no idea how to respond, I reply simply. "Thank you."

"Get settled, sweetheart." She touches my shoulder gently. "I'll be in the kitchen if you need anything." Her hand brushes over my forearm, feeling the ridges of scars, and she looks down, a sad frown marring her peaceful face. She squeezes my hand gently, looking back to me with tears in her eyes. "The Goddess doesn't want you to die, Alexa, or you wouldn't be here with me today. Even if you feel unworthy, it is an insult to her to throw your life away," she declares as she walks out, leaving me to let her words soak in.

The room does have great light, I'll give her that. With all the crazy bohemian clutter in the rest of the house, this room is plain by comparison. I unpack the handful of clothes I have into the dresser, then stare at its meager contents and fight the urge to cry. All my worldly possessions don't even fill one drawer. Nothing in that drawer is of any value; I've got nothing but my memories and the ink on my skin to remind me of my former life. I sit on the bed and run my finger over the butterflies adorning my arm. It's all I have left. It feels like a wisp of a dream in the horror that has been my life. Like it wasn't even real.

I curl up on the bed and cry over the loss of my best friend, her baby, and the love of a boy I'll never forget. The bed dips behind me, and I feel a hand on my shoulder.

"Oh, honey, I know the world is pushing you in the dirt right now, but life *is* beautiful, and every-thing *will* be okay."

"My best friend and her unborn child are dead because of me, and I lost my brother, my best friends, and my first love in a matter of days. I've got nothing left. Life is not beautiful. Life is pain."

"You'll see. Each day it will hurt a little less until one day you will be able to breathe without hurting." Lana brushes my hair out of my face. "Dinner is ready. Would you like to join us?"

I shake my head.

"This is your one get-out-of-dinner-free card. I'll give you today to adjust, but starting tomorrow, no more hiding, okay? Life is out there, not hiding in here wishing the world right again." She states all this kindly.

I nod. "Thank you, Lana."

"Get some rest, love. The weight of the world will feel a little lighter tomorrow." Then she leaves me alone for the rest of the night.

MORNING COMES, AND I FOLLOW THE SOUNDS OF voices into the kitchen.

Lana is sitting at the table in a yellow sundress with purple daisies all over it, her hair hanging over her shoulder in a long braid. She smiles at me over her mug. "Good morning, Lexi. Did you sleep well?"

I nod, then glance at the stove where a girl who must be her daughter is cooking bacon and eggs. It smells divine. She looks up at me, giving me a bright smile and waving at me with a spatula.

"Morning." She's stunning: long blonde hair pulled into a high ponytail, tall thin body with legs for days. Usually girls like her put me on edge, but she has a kind smile. She's dressed in a pair of ragged jean shorts with a T-shirt that says "I wish I was full of tacos instead of emotions." This makes me stifle a laugh.

"Do you like bacon, Lexi? Course you do, everyone loves bacon. Well, everyone except Lana," she jokes, rolling her eyes. I can't help but smile at her silliness.

"I don't eat loveable creatures, Rebekah," Lana replies, shaking her head.

"Pigs aren't that loveable. They're actually kind of mean. And really, it's their own fault. Maybe they shouldn't be so delicious if they didn't want to be eaten." She's laughing as she makes up two plates and slides one in front of me.

My stomach rumbles. I don't remember the last meal I ate. I devour the plate, mumbling a quick "Thank you."

Lana puts her bowl in the dishwasher before gathering her things off the counter. "Well, I'm off to work. What do you girls plan on doing today?"

"Last two weeks before school starts? I'm going to lie on the beach and do a whole lotta nothing!" Rebekah says with a smile. "Wanna come?"

"The beach?" I ask, excited. "Are we near the beach?"

She looks at me like I'm crazy. "Um, yeah... like a five-minute walk that way," she says, pointing over my shoulder. "So, you in?"

I smile and nod excitedly. "I've only been once before. It was the best day of my life," I say wistfully, remembering that perfect day.

"Awesome. Grab a suit and we'll have a lazy beach day."

"I don't have a swimsuit," I mumble dejectedly. "I don't have anything."

"Oh, shit, sorry. I guess you need some clothes and stuff. We can swing by the store and grab whatever you need, right, Lana? Easy fix."

"Of course. Your case worker mentioned the rest of your things wouldn't be mailed out for a week," Lana adds.

My things?

"I don't have any things. I thought everything was destroyed." Maybe I left something behind at the group home.

"I don't know, sweetie. She just said a box of your

things will arrive next week sometime. Okay, my lovelies, have a fun day. Make good choices, wear sunblock, and drink lots of water." She kisses us both on the cheek and glides out of the room in a wave of bright colors and flowing material. The bohemian queen.

"Where does she work, Rebekah?" I wonder aloud.

"She owns a hippie new-age bookshop down by the beach. And please, for the love of God, don't call me Rebekah. Only Lana does that. It's Bex," she says, holding out her hand.

I shake it. "How long have you been with Lana?"

"She legally adopted me when I was twelve, and she was my foster parent from when I was eight. She's wonderful, and I love her to bits, but she isn't my real mom." She pauses for a minute, as if in thought, then shakes her head.

———

I HELP CLEAN UP AFTER BREAKFAST.

"Ready to go, then?"

We head to a surf shop around the corner that has hundreds of bathing suits. I never had any money for clothes back home, so the options in front of me are making me a little cross-eyed.

Bex is not so shy. I think she might be the least shy person I've ever met. She picks out three suits for me, a couple pairs of shorts and flip-flops, and pushes me into a dressing room. Once I confirm it all fits, she snatches it all out of my hands and pays the girl behind the till as they make small talk about the weather. She's such a cool chick. She's happy and friendly to everyone she meets. I like her.

"That should last you until Lana takes us school shopping," she says as we walk back to the house to change and drop off the extra clothes.

"She won't be mad that you're spending all this money on me? I don't know how long I'll be around for."

This seems to shock her, as she stops dead.

"Lana isn't just some jerk foster parent. She takes this shit seriously. You aren't going anywhere. This is your home now for as long as you want it." She puts her hand on my shoulder. "Look, I know she seems flakey, but she's a wonderful person with a kind heart. You could do a lot worse than Lana. A lot worse," she states seriously, like she knows from experience.

"It's all so overwhelming. Within the last year, my

mom ran out on me, I lost my brother and my boyfriend, my best friend and her baby died, and I was shot twice. The whole life I was building for myself disappeared without a trace. A few months ago, I had everything: a family, a boyfriend, and friends who loved me. Now I have nothing. It's just hard for me to put faith in anyone." My confession leaves me embarrassed.

She nudges my shoulder with hers, and when I look up, she's smiling. "Come on. We need some sunshine. Nothing cures a bad day like sunshine on your face and your toes in the sand. Go get changed," she instructs, pushing me toward the stairs.

I dress quickly and am coming back down the stairs when I hear a wolf whistle.

"Damn, Lexi, looking hot!"

Laughing, I shake my head. "Shut up."

Bex loops her arm in mine. "Ha! I love you already. Best fake sister ever."

We walk out into the sunshine. After only a few minutes, I see the ocean ahead of us. My heart starts racing. "It's just as incredible as I remember."

She was right though: lying out in the sun, listening to the waves crash, makes me feel like my life is somehow in control.

This becomes our daily sun-worshiping ritual.

For the next week, Bex makes breakfast, Lana goes to work, we hang out on the beach, and Lana makes dinner. It's a calm, happy existence, and I try to enjoy its simplicity. But deep down I'm terrified that at any moment, the universe will backhand me and I'll end up in the gutter once again. It's only a matter of time.

———

I LIKE SPENDING TIME WITH BEX—SHE'S LOUD AND opinionated and incredibly bossy. She's more likely to give you an ass-kicking rather than a hug, but behind the wall of sass she's built around herself, I can tell there's a big loving heart.

Before going home today, Bex walks us over to a food truck with a sign stating it has the best burgers on the beach. We order a burger, fries, and iced tea each, then snag a nearby picnic table and sit across from each other.

When we lay out our meal, I look over at her questioningly. "Isn't it almost suppertime? Lana's making food."

"I don't know what you call that crap she cooks, but it most definitely isn't food." Taking a big bite of her burger, she says with a full mouth, "Mmm… now *this* is food."

I laugh and dig in.

"If you hate it so much, why do you eat it?" I ask after a couple bites.

"I love Lana, don't get me wrong. But she's a *vegan*." She says the word like she just announced Lana's an alien. "The last thing she needs is me telling her that her food sucks." *That's sweet.* "Which is why I offer to make breakfast every morning. To pitch in, of course. But also so I get at least one decent, animal protein-filled meal a day."

We're still sitting at the picnic table finishing our burgers and fries when a red convertible pulls in and parks close to us. A group of girls gets out, stopping in front of Bex. I smile up at them, thinking they must be Bex's friends from school, but the second I see the pinched bitch face, I know she isn't a friend. I've known this kind of girl my whole life. She's tall, blonde, dressed head to toe in designer clothes—her purse alone could have paid mine and Matty's rent for months.

I look at Bex, waiting for her snarky remarks that'll tear this little princess from hell to shreds, but her eyes are fixed on the ground. She doesn't even acknowledge that they're there.

"Aw, the loser foster kid got her own little pet loser foster kid," the girl out front says, and they all laugh at her stupid joke. Bex's submissive eyes never leave the ground.

I stare at the scene in shock. How can she just sit there while they treat her like that? The bitch then kicks Bex in the leg when she doesn't respond. They all laugh louder, and I'm raging, having reached my limit.

I stand up, coming face-to-face with this chick; I've faced down scarier bullies than this pampered princess. I turn on the fighter in me that I've kept locked away. Pulling out the pocketknife I always keep in my back pocket, I press it against her side as I lean in so no one can hear what I say to her.

"Next time you see her, keep walking, and don't even think about touching her again or I'll gut you like the pig you are." The girl is frozen in fear as I sit back down beside a shocked Bex and give them a sweet smile. "Y'all enjoy this incredible sunshine now. See you at school," I say in an incredibly sweet singsong voice.

"You're insane!" the girl says, grabbing her friends and fleeing in the direction of the ice cream shop.

"Yes I am, and don't you forget it." I burst out

laughing as soon as they're out of sight. Bex looks like she's in shock.

"What?" I say innocently, smiling at her. "Was I supposed to sit there and take it? I don't back down to anyone, Bex, especially entitled bitches like her. And you shouldn't either. You let one person walk all over you and it makes it so much easier for the next person," I say.

"She's always been like that. If I cry or talk back it gets worse. I hit her once and she called the cops!"

"Well, you have to do something."

"Oh, I do stuff," she suggests with a sly smile. "I'm like a passive-aggressive ninja with my revenge. It's epic, trust me." She walks past the girl's red car, looking over her shoulder to see if anyone is watching. "Keep watch for me. Let the master show you something special," she says, nodding for me to stand at the back of the car. I do, and she kneels like she's tying her shoelaces.

I look around. No one is paying attention to us, so I pull out my pocketknife and do a little ninja revenge of my own. I carve a word in small letters underneath her pretentious Mercedes symbol. Four little letters. "See you next Tuesday, bitch." She probably won't notice for weeks.

Just as I'm crossing my T, Bex walks up to me,

smiling, then looks at what I just did and shakes her head.

"Oh my God, you are so ghetto, Lexi! You're going to get us arrested! Come on," she says, pulling my arm, laughing hard.

"What did you do to her car?"

"Who, me?" she asks innocently before laughing. "Oh, I sprinkled a jar of lice in her car." She holds out a small jar in the palm of her hand, looking quite proud of herself.

I stop in my tracks. "Are you serious?" She nods. "Where on earth did you get a jar of lice?" My skin is crawling just thinking about it.

"You'd be amazed what you can find online," she admits with a smile.

I shake my head. "Teach me of your ninja ways, oh wise one," I say, bowing to her.

"Oh, the shenanigans we will have." She loops her arm in mine, and we carry on home.

NINE

WHEN WE ARRIVE, LANA IS STANDING AT THE STOVE making dinner, as usual.

"Hey, girls. The box of your things arrived, Lexi. I put it on your bed."

I race up there, unable to contain my excitement. I have no idea what could be in that box. Between my whole apartment getting trashed and the shooting, I thought I had nothing left.

I pull the lid off and inside sits my shoulder bag, stained in blood. I stare at it for a long time. That day feels like a nightmare, a distant memory—and a foggy one at that. But seeing my bag, knowing those dark marks are blood, brings it all rushing back.

I finally get the courage to touch it. Pulling it out, I dump the contents on my bed. My camera falls out, and I feel like I just regained a piece of my soul. I never realized how much I'd missed hiding behind my camera. I roll it in my hands; it doesn't look like it was damaged. I turn it on and am shocked to see the battery isn't dead. The screen tells me there are twenty-two pictures on its memory card. I start to click through them but freeze when I come to a photo of Elise and Marco. He's standing behind her holding her hands on her round belly, and they're both radiating pure joy.

I drop to the floor and start crying, staring at that perfect moment frozen in time. She's alive and well. In every picture I flip through, her radiant smile shines through. It's like a salve to my burn and a knife in my heart at the same time. I want to crawl into that perfect world where she still lives and stay forever. She deserved so much more.

"Did you find it?" Lana peeks in to see what was delivered. Seeing me collapsed and crying, clinging to my camera, she sits down next to me and pulls me into a hug. She rocks me and hums a little song.

After a few minutes, she leans back, brushing the hair out of my face. She gives me a sad smile and says, "Show me."

I nod and turn the camera toward her so she can

see. "Her name is Elise. She is… was my best friend," I say, pointing to the photos.

"Was? Where is she now?"

"She's dead. We were both shot the same night. She didn't make it." I'm sobbing now. "She deserves to live so much more than I do. It was my fault. I shouldn't have gone back there. She told me not to, said it wasn't safe, but I was worried about Matty and I wanted my stuff. She was killed because of my stupidity," I say angrily. I throw the box across the room.

"Hey, don't do that. Don't act like all the bad things in this world are your fault. You know in your heart it isn't true. Bad things happen all the time to good people. Don't turn your back on your life because you think someone else is more worthy of it. Honor her by living, by remembering how she lit up your life. Don't stop loving the people who leave us. I know it feels impossible now, but I promise it will get easier," she says, pulling me into a hug.

I sob uncontrollably in her arms. "I feel so lost and alone in the world," I confess, holding on to her.

"You aren't lost. You just don't know where you are until you take that first step. That first step into the rest of your life." She pulls back so she can see my face. "Don't forget them. Bring them with you. Carry them in your heart."

"Thank you, Lana." I sniffle. "You've been so amazing."

"Rebekah and I love having you here, Lexi. I hope you know that this is your home now. I know my sister wasn't any kind of parent to you. She's been running from her own demons since we were kids. That's no excuse for what she put you through, but you need to know we're your family. We're here for you, whatever you need," she says, hugging me again.

"Will you help me find Matty?" I ask.

"Of course. We'll see what we can find out. Did you know we met once before? You were this little wobbly three-year-old. Matty was around five, I think. Erica showed up a few days before Christmas, no word or warning, with you two in tow. Lord, were we surprised to meet you! Mama nearly had a heart attack, finding out she was a grandmother. I never saw her so happy. She rushed out shopping, bought nearly the whole toy store for you two. We were determined to give you a great Christmas. I was so excited to be an auntie.

"When we got back from shopping, you and Matty were alone in the house. Erica had taken off on Christmas Eve. You were with us all through

New Year's. She showed up a few days after New Year's, just walked in, picked you up, and walked out. Matty followed like he always did. We should have stopped her. Goddess knows I wanted to stop her, but she was your mom. I'm so sorry we didn't. But I'm here now, and I'm so glad I found you."

We're both in a pool of tears. How is it possible that I love this woman more than my own mother and I've known her five minutes?

"That's a very cool camera," she says after we pull ourselves together.

I nod. "It is. Matty got it for me. I love taking pictures."

"An artist, I knew it. I felt this incredible artistic vibe coming off you the moment I laid eyes on you," she says, smiling down at me.

I can't help but laugh. She's a trip.

"We'll see what we can find out about your brother tomorrow. Come down for dinner, and you and Bex can pretend you didn't already eat. Then you can tell me what had you cackling like demons up to no good when you walked in the door."

My eyes go wide a moment, wondering how much she knows.

"Hope you got those girls good this time," she says, shaking her head as she walks out of my room.

I glance down at the camera and scroll through a few more until I get to the one I know is there. Noah's smiling face comes on the small screen, and I stare into his dark eyes. I miss him so much my heart aches, and I allow one tear to fall. I run my fingers over his lips, remembering what they felt like.

"I love you," I whisper to him, hoping by some miracle he can hear me wherever he is.

I turn off the camera, placing it on my night-stand. I'm looking forward to spending half the night staring into his eyes. At least I can be grateful I have these memories of a life I had once, a life full of love and hope for the future. It'll have to be enough to carry me through.

"Until we meet again," I whisper into the dark.

DINNER WAS... EDIBLE, I GUESS. I'M STARTING TO TIRE of Lana's vegan ways. Some dishes are tasty, but most are missing one key ingredient—meat. But like Bex, I love Lana and respect her enough to eat the food she's made for us.

Bex tells her what she did to that girl's car, and Lana laughs. We don't mention what I did, since it's illegal and aggressive, two things Lana disagrees with.

Bex and I clean up after dinner together and then go up to her room. We listen to music and watch YouTube videos. I show her the pictures of my friends on the small camera screen. All of a sudden her eyes light up. She jumps off her bed and starts rummaging through her desk, bringing a cord over. She plugs one end into my camera and the other into her computer, then starts clicking and typing with a big smile, nodding occasionally.

"What are you doing?" I ask.

"Just wait," she says, holding up a finger. "You'll love it, I promise." Then she disconnects the camera, hands it back to me, and runs out of the room.

I start playing with settings on my camera and snap a few pictures of her bedroom before she comes running back. She's hiding her hands behind her back, and a huge smile is plastered on her face.

"What?"

She thrusts her hands out and in them are photographs, the ones from my camera. All of them on photo paper, in perfect detail.

"You printed them? Thank you," I say, tears clogging my throat.

She just shrugs and sits back down.

"If they're that important to you, you should be able to see them whenever you want," she says, pointing to a picture on her nightstand I'd never noticed. It's of a woman in a flowing white dress in a field of daisies; she looks so much like Bex that it can only be her mother. She picks up the frame, kisses it, and then turns it to me with a wave of her hand.

"Mom, this is Lexi. She's my new sister. Lexi, this is my mom, Danika. I've told her all about you." She places the frame back in its spot, adjusting it just so before turning back to me. "She died when I was eight. I still talk to her every day though. I just thought maybe having the pictures to talk to will help you too,"

"It's incredible. Thank you," I say, reaching across and pulling her into a hug as happy tears flow.

Later, I lay out all the pictures on my bed. It feels like decades ago, not months. I ask Lana for some tape and arrange the pictures on the wall, making peace with my loss. Bex is right, it feels better to see their faces and talk to them. To remind myself that they were real, that maybe Noah and I can overcome this separation. If only he would talk to me.

Lying in bed that night, I send out a prayer to Lana's Goddess for Noah and me to find each other. That this won't be the end of us. My heart breaks thinking of Noah and Marco hurting over the death of Elise and the baby. Marco mourning the death of his young wife and unborn child. I yearn to hear Noah's voice, but the number has been disconnected.

Bex left her laptop in my room, and I can't resist the urge to search the internet for them.

After starting it up, I search for Noah King, then Elise and Marco Heart, finding nothing on Facebook. Then I search Matthew Young. Nothing. Well, not nothing, but there are about three hundred Matt Youngs. How on earth will I find them?

I send another prayer out to keep Matty safe. My heart is broken, and the shattered pieces have been scattered on the wind. I need to find them.

The next weekend, Lana invites her boyfriend, John, over for dinner. There's a storm of nervousness brewing in my stomach at the thought of him being anything like Erica's boyfriends. I shrink into myself, avoiding eye contact for the duration of dinner. John tries to engage me in conversation, but my throat closes and I give one-word answers to anything he asks. I push food around my plate long enough for everyone else to finish eating before I excuse myself from the table and hide in my room.

Bex comes in a little while later and sits on the

edge of my bed. "What's going on, Lexi? What happened down there?"

"I just don't want to ruin what I have here. When my mom brought guys around, if they looked at me for even a second, she would flip out and hit me."

"God, Lexi. Do you really think John and Lana are like that? I've known John for ten years, and he has never once made me feel uncomfortable or unsafe in any way. You need to trust us. We would never let anything bad happen to you."

"You're right. I'm such a mess." I get up and go into the living room where Lana and John are sitting having a glass of wine. They look up at me when I enter, and my eyes well with tears. "I'm sorry, guys. I have a hard time opening up to new people. It's just hard to change a lifetime of thinking all people are bad. I'm so sorry, John."

"You don't owe me an apology, Alexa. I understand how life can make you feel like nothing good could happen. Lana has told me a little about your history. Anyone who's lived through that would need to be guarded. It's self-preservation. I love Lana and Rebekah with my whole heart and hope that once you get to know me, you'll let me in as you've let them in. I'm not so bad. Promise." He offers a small smile.

"We love you, Lexi. Whatever you need to feel more comfortable, let us know," Lana says, hugging me.

I squeeze her tightly. "I love you too, Lana. I can't thank you enough for taking me in."

TEN

IT CAME.

The make-or-break moment of my entire existence. An acceptance letter... or rejection from the art school of my dreams. Only an hour away from Lana's, Bex and I will relocate this summer, if I'm accepted. I've been staring at this envelope for an hour, unable to face whatever future it holds within.

Their photography program is the best in the state, and I desperately want in. I've never wanted something so badly in my entire life. I want to work with these brilliant people who already change the way we see things with their art. I knew it was the place for me when I started reading about the courses they offered. It inspired me. I can see my future laid out before me. Being accepted would mean everything to me, but rejection... I'm terrified what that would do to me.

I've worked so hard over the last year, and now, with the help of my teachers and Lana, I've got a shot. I know I do. Bex has been accepted into the veterinarian program at a school close by. Now it's my turn to grab my future with both hands. I just need to open this letter.

I wasn't going to apply, but in the end, Lana forced me into it. I didn't dare believe I could fulfill my dreams. I was raised to be invisible, that the things I wanted didn't matter and no one really cared about my dreams. Everything always felt so out of reach.

The portfolio I submitted had a collection of pictures of Noah, Matty, Elise, and Marco with the story of my life and my trials and how my camera and photography became an outlet for my healing. A way to hold on to my past and give me the strength to reach for a future I never thought possible. Lana cried when she read it and said it was perfect.

Bex comes through the door, spotting me sitting at the kitchen table, chin resting on my folded arms, staring at the envelope dreams are made of. "Oh my God, is that what I think it is?"

"That depends. Do you think it's good news or bad?"

"You haven't opened it yet?"

"No," I say incredulously, like it's a bomb that could detonate at any moment, destroying all my hopes for the future.

She strides over, picks it up, and within seconds has it opened and is reading what it says.

"You're in!" she screams. We jump around together excitedly.

"Yes!" I say, grabbing the paper out of her hands. There it is in black-and-white. Come fall, I'll be a college student, a photographer. All I need to do is get through these last two months of high school.

"ALEXA RAINE."

The sound of my name ringing through the speakers sends a chill over my skin. I became Alexa Raine a few months after Lana took me in. She officially adopted me, leaving behind any attachment I had to Erica Young. I no longer belong to her, I belong to myself, and I was thrilled when Lana asked if she could make it official. Honestly, I jumped at the chance to make a change and finish out my senior year as Lexi Raine. To separate myself from the noose Erica kept around my neck.

Against all odds, I made it. This is it.

One step at a time, I walk toward the stage where Principle Vicars is standing, ready to shake my hand. All I've got to do is walk up there, get my diploma, and walk across the stage. On the other side is my future. I'm really hoping I can do this without passing out.

Come on, Lexi, you can do this. It's only like fifteen steps, maybe twenty. Just walk up there, in front of all these people, shake her hand, take your diploma, and walk off.

Simple things that I'm capable of, but I feel like all the air is being sucked out of the room.

As I step up one, two, three steps, my breath quickens and my palms get sweaty. Why am I so nervous? I've been looking forward to today. I'm eighteen and out of high school. I can go wherever I want and be whoever I want to be. The first step to becoming my own person.

Lana and John cheering my name and hollering like I just won an Oscar and not a high school diploma snaps me out of my daydream. I scan the audience for their friendly faces. It doesn't take long because Lana is holding up a sign with "Congrats, Bex and Lex" in glittery letters. It brings a smile to my face. Their support and love carry me across that stage and to the other side where Bex is waiting to envelop me in a big hug.

"This is it, Lex. We're free from this place. We can do anything we want."

A shrill laugh comes from behind me. Britney, the entitled swine, has to get one last dig in. "Yeah, you can do anything you want. You could work at Walmart or Hooters." Then she glances down at my chest with a smirk. "Walmart it is." She turns to snicker with her three minions behind her.

I clench my fists, nails digging into my skin. *I will not murder her. I will not murder her.*

I shoot Bex a wink before she steps up to respond to the evil cow. "Well, Hooters is better than the future you have ahead of you. Trapping some premed date-rapist mama's boy into marriage. He'll never get over his premature ejaculation, but that won't stop him from banging interns and nurses at the hospital working those late shifts while you sit at home, hating yourself and your life a little more with every bottle of wine you drink, all because you're a shallow cunt with no soul. Enjoy being a bitter, washed-up divorcée by thirty."

Britney just stares in utter shock at the sting of that epic burn. It's like you can watch every miserable moment of the dream life she wanted get tainted by Bex's words. Bex slips her arm around my shoulders, steering us away from any further drama.

"Alexa Raine, you ignore that mean-ass ho and let's celebrate the rest of our lives!" she yells, high-fiving a random classmate. She's always able to brush aside any bullying and harsh words thrown at her and walk away smiling.

I just can't stop the words from penetrating my armor. I never could. If someone says something hurtful, even as a joke, it digs into my soul like a burr, and there it waits like a dark cloud on a sunny day, ready to ruin a good thing.

Thankfully I'm in control of my cutting, but on my darkest days, the temptation is still there. It may always be there, but it isn't enough to push me over the edge.

Lana and John come over in a whirl of photo snapping and hugs. "I'm so proud of my girls!" Lana can't hold back her tears as she looks at us. "So grown up. You girls ready for dinner? Our reservations at Positano Grill aren't for an hour."

Bex cuts in before I can answer. "We'll meet you

there. We just have a few proper goodbyes we haven't said yet."

I watch her, confused, but don't interrupt whatever she has planned. We send them off to hold our table at our favorite restaurant while we enact whatever twisted plot Bex has up her sleeve this time. I know Britney's dig will not go unpunished.

"What's the plan, Bex? We going to dump a bucket of pig's blood on her?"

"Ew, no! Lana would kill us if we did something so barbaric."

"Color her car in jiffy marker? Banana in her gas tank? I think we still have some fish guts in the freezer from last time. Oh, how about dog poop on the floor mats of her car again? That's my favorite. She stank all day." I chuckle to myself remembering everyone's disgusted face as Britney walked down the hall. It was brilliant.

She looks at me longingly, batting her eyes and clutching her chest. "You're the she to my nanigans, I'm proud to call you sister. No, this is our final attack. We can't do some tired old prank we've already done three times this year," she states as she rummages in her purse. "Aha! There it is." She pulls out a large Ziploc bag full of glitter. Upon closer inspection, I see it's a mix of regular glitter and penis glitter.

"What are you going to do with that bag of glitter dicks, Bex?"

"We, Lexi. The word is we. We are going to pour it into the air vents in her car, of course." Like it should have been obvious.

I burst out laughing. "Lord, I love your crazy ass." She may take shit from Britney, but she gives twice as good as she gets. Revenge is like an art form for Bex. I'm just along for the laughs.

Instantly, we go into stealth mode. Back-to-back, with our finger guns at the ready, we look around before running to the parking lot, bobbing and weaving through people and cars like spies on the run. We spot our target: a cherry-red Mercedes convertible, license plate DADZGRL. She never puts the top up unless it's raining, no matter how many times we've messed with her car. It's like she's asking for it.

"Keep watch."

I nod as Bex pulls a funnel out of her bag of wonders. "You're like freaking Mary Poppins with that thing."

"Practically perfect. Sounds about right."

"Hurry up before someone sees." Britney is

having a photo shoot on stage with her parents, but she won't be long.

Bex works methodically, filling each vent she can reach, emptying the massive bag. "Glitter, the gift that keeps on giving."

We meet up with Lana and John for dinner at our favorite Italian restaurant after the revenge hoopla is over.

"Come on, Lex. It's one little party. Please come with me." Bex has been hounding me nonstop, trying to convince me to go to this awful grad party I want no part of. I grew up in a drug-infested party house. I'm aware of the dangers of letting my guard down around drunk men.

"I can't think of anything worse than fighting off drunk teenage boys as they drink until they puke or pass out."

"Don't you want some cute boy getting all up in your business?" She reaches out and mocks grabbing my boobs with a laugh.

"Ew, no!" I slap her grabby hands away, laughing.

"I do! Come on," Bex insists. "I need to experience at least one high school party or I'll become some crazy deprived old lonesome cat lady. And probably a hoarder. I don't want to be on my deathbed regretting not going to this party, letting my youth slip away without any fun."

"Good lord," I say, rolling my eyes. "Being young and reckless is overrated. Give me adulthood and independence. And you know damn well that we'll be the coolest cat ladies on the block." I'm an old soul; give me peace and calm and I'm happy as a clam. Is that a saying? Are clams happy? How on earth would you tell?

"Please, I need to see Britney's face. It'll be the perfect way to say goodbye."

"Fine," I relent, and Bex squeals and hugs me excitedly.

I hate high school parties. Over the last ten months, Bex has dragged me to three, each time swearing it will be the last. I put up a fight, but in the end, we always go. She's an unstoppable force of nature, and I love her for it. Honestly, it's not so bad, and we always have fun together. Unless Britney's there. Then we let loose the shenanigans.

Bex and I have made that girl's life hell just as much as she has with us. It's a delicate balance and one we take very seriously.

. . .

THE NIGHT PROGRESSES EXACTLY AS EXPECTED WITH Britney showing up with her skin blotchy from scrubbing the glitter. She knows it was us but for some reason avoids verbally attacking us.

Bex decides to get legendarily drunk. One second she's talking with friends in the kitchen, and then boom, the next she's ten Jell-O shots in. Ten! I pry the tray from her hands and sit her on the couch while I run to get her a glass of water. I'm having a decent enough time until I spot Bex over Greg the pig's shoulder as she drifts in and out of consciousness.

"Oi, hands off," I call out to him. He locks eyes with me for a second, but, clearly not taking my demand seriously, he carries her out of the room while smacking her ass, much to the amusement of his friends. They disappear down a hallway to the right of the kitchen.

Looks like I'm going to have to kick some ass.

Pushing my way through the throngs of party people, I go slowly at first but quickly turn aggressive when they don't get out of my way. This is exactly why I didn't make any friends with these people. Not one of them cares what's going on. I swear I'll kill him if he touches her.

Opening each door in the hall, I find them on the

third try. My heart drops at the sight in front of me. Bex lies limp on the bed. He's trying to take off her shirt.

I jump on his back, screaming, punching him wildly. Why do guys think they have the right to any woman's body?

Britney comes in the room, laughing. "You'll pay for what you did to my car, bitch."

"Aw, we thought you liked taking dicks to the face. Pretty sure that's what we read on the bathroom wall, right, Bex?"

"You wrote that!"

"Doesn't mean it's not true, dickface." I can't hold back my snicker.

Bex chuckles. "Dickface." Pointing at Britney, she then pukes over the side of the bed. Wiping the puke with her sleeve, she slurs, "What's going on?"

"You're a lousy cocktease is what's happening," Greg spits.

My fist flies out of nowhere, connecting with his face and causing him to double over, squealing in pain.

Britney takes a pathetic swing at me, snapping Bex out of her drunken state as she launches herself at Britney, screaming like a banshee. Us versus them in an epic battle of the ages. More people rush into the room as our fight escalates. Bex and I are taking on four of the nastiest bitches at our school with blood and mayhem. We keep swinging and pulling hair until the flashing lights arrive and everyone starts to scatter.

When the cops enter the room, Britney has hold of my hair and I'm swinging at her face. Bex is now sitting on the floor throwing anything she can get her hands on at Lacy, Britney's friend. The police break up the party, lining Bex, Britney, and me up against their cars, all messy hair, underage drinking and fighting. No shocker that we're thrown in the back of the cop cars. Happy graduation, indeed.

Sitting in the dark, waiting for them to drive us to the station, panic sets in. "Lana is going to kill us," I say to Bex.

Holding a paper towel to her bleeding nose, she side-eyes me, raising an eyebrow. "Lana will bail us out."

"I'm sorry I got us in a fight."

"Are you kidding me? This has become my favorite high school memory ever. We kicked some serious ass in there," Bex says, holding up her hand for a high five. We both laugh at the chaos that was our last high school shenanigan. She curls up with her head in my lap. "Hard to believe a year ago you were a stranger to me, and now we're sisters for life. Life's funny that way. Love you, Lex."

"Love you, Bex."

She goes quiet, and I know she's fallen asleep. I watch her sleep and can't help but smile. She's so much fun and lightness. So much like Elise. I feel like in some strange way, Elise sent me Lana and Bex, knowing how much I needed them. How much their love would help me heal.

Since no charges were laid and it was grad night, they let us off with a warning, though it takes Lana three hours to get us out. I'm pretty sure she let us stew for a while on purpose. She turns a blind eye to most of our shenanigans, but this she won't be happy about. Especially Bex being drunk and fighting.

Sure enough, the concern on Lana's face when she comes into view says it all. Her eyes are red and puffy, and I know she's been crying. Guilt swells in my stomach. I did this to her. I could have stopped tonight from happening.

"Sorry," I say, leading Bex to Lana's car.

She shakes her head, taking the other side of Bex and get her lanky ass in the back seat.

The drive home is quiet, aside from Bex's snores. I keep looking over at Lana, trying to think of something to say, to gauge how angry she is. "Please say something."

"There's nothing to say. You're adults now, and your first night out, you messed up. I'm not thrilled you girls resorted to violence, but I believe in my heart you stand by your reasons. I hope you had fun, but more importantly, I hope you learned your lesson and this doesn't happen again."

LYING IN BED, I LET THE EVENTS OF TONIGHT SINK IN. Though I didn't get drunk or do drugs, I acted out violently and got arrested. How am I any different than my mother if this is how I control myself?

I clench my fists and close my eyes, trying to block out the Erica Young commentary running through my mind, calling me useless trash and a full arsenal of insults on repeat. I drag in a shaky breath as images of a knife cutting my arm flashes in my mind. *I will not cut. I will not let memories make me hurt myself.* The butterflies etched on my arm always calm my breathing and bring me back to myself. *Live for Elise. Accept the things I can't change, and never forget how far I've come.*

In the quiet darkness of the night, Noah is never far from my heart or mind. My heart aches for his touch, his voice. Anything to keep him close. I have my pictures from last summer that decorate my walls, but I need more. I wonder if there will ever be a time when I don't long for his touch. It's a year later, and I know in my heart he was my soul mate. I will find him, even if it's just to say I'm sorry for my part in Elise's death. I need closure or reconciliation. I feel incomplete without him.

ELEVEN

THE FIRST WEEK AFTER GRADUATION GOES BY IN A flash of planning. Bex and I've been searching for apartments and jobs in the area close to the art school—*my* art school. I give a secret little squeal at the fact that I'm going to be learning everything there is to know about photography. This is really happening.

Sadly, the excitement bubble pops when we realize rent in the places close to the school is atrocious and we'll have to work three full-time jobs on top of school just to cover it.

"How are we going to do this, Bex?"

With a sigh, she flops back onto the couch. "I have no freaking idea. We'll just have to search farther away. Your commute will suck, but at least we'll be able to afford to eat."

Lana and John walk in carrying grocery bags. "Girls, there's more in the car. Can you grab them please?"

We amble out to collect the rest of the bags and help put everything away.

"What's got you two looking so miserable?" John asks, popping a grape in his mouth.

Bex hops up on the counter, looking defeated. "All the places near school are way overpriced. It's like they're specifically gouging money from students."

John and Lana exchange a strange look. "Lana, I think it's time we tell them."

My heart sinks, automatically jumping to a million terrible conclusions. "Is everything okay?"

"Come sit down, girls. John and I have some news to share." We take seats in the living room and wait with bated breath for their news. Lana looks at us and says, "We've sold the house."

Bex jumps up, outraged. "What? Why? You're leaving us?"

"Rebekah, you're eighteen. You're both going away to school. There is just no sense in me keeping the house when we plan to travel for a few years."

"I guess that makes sense." I'm trying to understand their need to move on after we move away, but I can't help feeling a little like we're being abandoned. "It's going to be weird to not have you and this place to come back to."

John takes out a piece of paper from his pocket and hands it to Bex. She opens it and we see it's a realtor listing for a cute little two-story house. We stare at them, confused. "Did you buy this house? Where is it? I thought you wanted to travel?"

"It's located between your schools, only five blocks. It's our graduation gift to you both."

"Are you serious? Oh my God, I love you so much. Thank you! This is incredible." Bex jumps up, screaming and hugging Lana and John.

I sit there in shock. This can't be real. They bought us a house. My own mother abandoned me, and these two incredible people love us so much they bought us a house.

Lana's voice snaps me out of my fog. "Lexi, honey, are you okay?"

"No one has ever done anything like this for me, Lana. It's too much," I say, weeping.

She pulls me into a hug, and everyone's cheeks are wet with tears.

John clears his throat, wiping tears from his

cheeks. "We love you girls so much, and there was no way we could go away without knowing you'd be okay. Once we saw how much rent was going to be, our minds were set. This way you will always have somewhere safe to call home and we have somewhere to stop by when we tire of traveling. It isn't anything spectacular, but I know my girls can make it a lovely home."

"And it has a guest house out back that you could turn into a studio," Lana adds.

"Thank you. I love you guys." I can't stop the flow of tears. I glance at Bex, who is a crying mess too.

"We love you too. We're so proud of you both," John says, choking up again.

"We have so much faith in our girls. We know you'll build a wonderful life there," Lana adds.

WE SPEND THE NEXT WEEK PACKING UP OUR LIVES into boxes. Lana and John put most of their things in storage, but the rest we load into a moving truck and drive the hour and a half to our new home and life.

The house is even more adorable in person. It has a quirky charm with bright colors, like Lana's house, and the neighborhood looks safe and welcoming. After a few hours, we're exhausted from unpacking.

We grab some takeout and have our last meal together as a family for a while. Lana and John are set to leave tomorrow on a three-month tour of Italy. It all feels like it's happening so fast.

We settle in, surrounded by boxes, and spend our last night together laughing and sharing stories.

The morning is full of quiet reflection. Goodbyes are coming, giving an air of sadness to our new happy home. We know they'll be back soon enough, but saying goodbye to the only parents who have ever loved me is breaking my heart. When we arrive at the airport, there is no hope of stopping the river of tears, even though in my heart, I know Lana isn't leaving me in the true sense, and she'll only be just a phone call away. She has been the most loving and wonderful person I know; she has the truest heart, so full of light and love.

"I'm a better person today because I was dropped on your doorstep."

"Oh, honey, you are a kind-hearted, wonderful girl who deserves nothing short of a happy life. I'm the one who was blessed with you both. When I was told I couldn't have kids, I thought part of me would always be missing until you girls brought so much light into my life. You changed my life and answered a lifetime of prayers and wishes. Because of you, I got to be a mom."

With one last group hug, we send them on their adventure with promises to keep in touch and stay out of trouble. Arm in arm, Bex and I walk out to our car.

"And then there were two," she says through tears.

"Come on, sis, let's go home."

TWELVE

FOUR YEARS LATER...

THE PHONE RINGING SNAPS ME OUT OF THE WORK
trance I've been in for hours, hunched over the table
going over the contact sheets from my latest shoot.
Stretching my arms above my head, I pick up the
phone.

"Alexa Raine Photography." God, I love the sound
of that. I'm a professional photographer with a full
booking calendar. It's been a lot of hard work, but
it's a dream come true.

Mrs. Neilson continues to tell me all about
another idea she has for her daughter Sarah's
engagement shoot this weekend. Sarah is a close

friend. She, Bex, and I used to work together in college. Lord have mercy, this must be her twentieth call in the last month, each with something new she saw on Pinterest. She's footing the bill, so I tell her how interesting her ideas are. Poor Sarah, her mom must be driving her nuts. I appreciated the bride-to-be giving me the heads-up that her mother is so overbearing. It's an exciting time for all of them, so I try to accommodate her as much as I can.

After hanging up, I take out the contact sheet for the show, reminding myself that I need to go downstairs to start the placement and lighting in the gallery. The anxiety over a show is almost too much for me to bear. Everything needs to be perfect. I only do a couple a year, thank the Goddess. The rest of my time is spent meeting clients and working on their individual needs, and in my spare time, I plan my next show. It's nerve wracking to listen to people talk about my work, but it's important for the artist to be on-site to shake hands and justify them spending their hard-earned money on my work. It's been a blessing that my work has done as well as it has.

I graduated from the photography program with a wealth of knowledge and a massive portfolio.

According to my professors, my work is thought-provoking, and I have a talent for evoking emotion.

My latest show is entitled *Graceful Sacrifice* and debuts tomorrow. I spent months with the local ballet company, documenting their struggle and dedication to their art. The pain dancers endure is astonishing to me, all for the love of dance. The photos I chose are a mixture of the grace and effort-less beauty of their movement countered by the agony of the craft, the way they bruise and bleed for their art. I can't stop looking at my selections and wondering if I picked the best of the best. Are they lit perfectly? Did I do them justice? I'm constantly critiquing my work, trying to make it better not only for my clients but for myself.

I'M SO GRATEFUL LANA GAVE US A HOUSE. I'VE transformed the guest house out back into my own studio over a small gallery to display my work. It's really given me a chance to stand out in this industry.

Bex walks in carrying two coffees and a bag of what I hope is some sort of sugary pastry in one hand. The other hand is cradling a kitten that was abandoned two nights ago outside the shelter she volunteers at. She drops the coffee and snacks on my desk, takes one look at the sheets I've been hunched over, and rolls her eyes. "You picked the best ones. They're lit so perfectly. It's heaven itself shining down on them. Stop already. Every year you turn into this insanely obsessive perfectionist. You are amazing, your work is amazing, and the show will be brilliant."

"Love you, Bex. What did you bring me?"

"Caffeine, sugar, icing, and grease. What else do artists eat for breakfast?"

"Self-loathing and neurosis?"

"Shut up! Did I miss Mrs. Neilson's call?"

I start laughing. "Just hung up. She wanted to let me know that if I cut a heart-shaped hole in cardboard and place it over my camera lens, it will play with the lighting and make precious little hearts everywhere."

"She does realize you're a professional and went to school for this stuff? That maybe, just maybe, you know more than her?"

"Customer is always right. Just a few more days and we won't have to see her again."

"Until the wedding day, and all the babies Sarah has."

I groan at the thought of a lifetime with Mrs. Neilson's phone calls.

"How's the tiniest fur baby ever?" I ask, petting Newt between his ears. He's so small.

"He's doing great. He needed me to bring him home last night. I couldn't leave him there all alone. I'll swing by the office on our way to the club."

I roll my eyes. Left to her own devices, Bex would have a menagerie of animals that would shame a zoo. Each one is precious to her, and she has a constant companion of the furry—and sometimes not-so-furry—variety.

***

BEX AND I WORKED AT SHOTS, A CLUB DOWNTOWN, through college. Working there was a blessing and a curse; we made killer money, but like all bars, it's not the best place to meet nice guys. Once we finished school, we were ready to move on. But for some reason, that didn't stop us from going there once a week to let loose.

Three tequila shots later, I spot Christopher sitting at the end of the bar, a collection of college girls around him, looking smart, sexy, and predatory—the perfect trap. He's handsome and says all the right things to get in your pants or get you drunk and convince you to pose naked for his *art*. He's charming and is dripping in old money. I can see why he attracts the girls—hell, I know from experience. He's the cautionary tale we're told but never listen to, an initiation into the world of handsome, manipulative artists.

I met Christopher, a photographer, during school when I interned for him for a semester. He was incredibly knowledgeable and charming. At the time, he made me feel like I was his greatest muse, that there was something special about me that lit up his creativity, that getting drunk would help the creative juices flow, that it was *my* idea to strip for him. He tried his damnedest to get in my pants but settled for the half-naked pictures. My refusal to have sex with him only spurs his interest, but I've seen behind the curtain. What other girls see as charming and professional I now see as classic entitled douchebag syndrome. He locks eyes with me and winks. Crap, he's headed this way.

"Alexa, looking sexy as hell tonight. When are you going to let me show you how exquisite we could be together?"

"When you wake up as something other than a metrosexual hipster douchebag," I say to his face.

He just smiles like the Cheshire cat and walks away with his arm slung around his latest victim.

Sadly, my constant rejection and verbal abuse haven't deterred him from showing up at Shots periodically to chat me up. I know what he wants, what he always wants. Some nights, I can feel my resolve wavering. I'm so damn tired of being alone. Bex keeps pushing me to date or at least hook up with someone, but the thought of anyone but Noah still makes my skin crawl. Bex says sex is good for the soul, but the only thing my soul needs is a strong cup of coffee in one hand and my camera in the other.

And Noah, my heart whispers.

Five years that I haven't heard from him or my brother. Five long years of not knowing if they're alive. And not a day goes by that I don't think about them and the day they both disappeared from my life.

"Earth to Lexi." Bex's voice snaps me out of my thoughts.

When I meet her gaze, she has a sad smile on her beautiful face; she knows where my mind was wandering, where it always wanders. We have a silent conversation: *"You good?" "Yeah, I'm good."*

This really is the best way to spend a night. Any time spent with her is a blast. We dance our little hearts out, and at one point we end up behind the bar pouring shots and mixing drinks with Sarah and Nate, like old times, then shaking our asses until the wee hours of the morning.

I WAKE UP AROUND NOON, ODDLY PROUD THAT I didn't wake up with a hangover. I shuffle downstairs to the kitchen, taking my coffee and bagel with me out back to my studio. Having the studio at our house has been a lifesaver. I could never thank Lana and John enough for giving us this house. I love being able to lose myself in my work whenever the urge takes over, and not having to rent a studio space is a money saver.

Bex wanders out an hour or so later, bringing the coffee press with her, knowing I'll need a refill. "What's on the docket today, boss?"

She works as my assistant on most of my shoots but also as my favorite model. She's stunning, and her photos always sell for top dollar.

"Obsessing over the show. Sarah's engagement photo shoot is tomorrow. I was also reading up on an idea for the next show. I'd like to do something about scars and tattoos, how people use ink to heal old wounds. Mine have talked me off the ledge more than a few times."

"That's a great idea. Where do we start?"

"Talk to tattoo parlors, I guess. See if they have any clients who might be interested in telling their story through photographs."

"I'm on it. I'll book a few consults for the week after your show." She sits in the office chair, starting up the computer. "There's an email from the PI, Lex."

"Really?" No news is always bad news when it comes to trying to find my brother, so any time the investigator messages me, I get excited. "What does it say?" I ask, leaning over her shoulder to read. "Shit, he just wants more money? He hasn't even found anything yet."

"Don't get mad, but how long are you going to keep this up? You've been paying this guy for a year with no leads. Maybe he's ripping you off. I mean, how would you even know if he were?"

I sigh. "I don't understand how it can be this hard to find him."

"Maybe he changed his last name like you? I'm not saying you should stop. I just worry about you getting your hopes up only to be disappointed."

"I know it's a long shot. And you're right. This guy has had a year of my money and hasn't found anything. Maybe it's time to finally give up." My shoulders slump; saying the words causes a stab of pain in my heart. I don't want to give up. I just don't know what else to do.

"Like Lana always says, 'Once you stop looking for something, it usually finds you,'" she mimics with a hopeful smile. I give her a quick hug and try to go back to work, feeling defeated.

Over the years, I've tried to search for Matty on my own, but it's impossible. The only tool I have up my sleeve is the internet, and that hasn't gotten me anywhere either. There are too many people out there in the world, and he doesn't seem to want to be found.

Of course, it has occurred to me that he might be trying to find me as well, so I joined Facebook and added Young to my profile name on the off chance he might be looking for me.

More than anything, I want to reach out to Noah, but what could I say besides "I miss you. Sorry I got your sister killed"? Anyway, his mom was clear about not wanting me in his life. I have to respect that.

Too much time has passed anyway. I wonder if he really was as I remember him or if it was young love that made him shine like perfection. His kindness and love still live within me. I still feel him on my lips and fingertips, his memory a vivid fantasy that I live in every day. Could his memory be skewed by years of longing, or was he truly my soul mate?

Either way, he's become the standard I measure guys against—and they fall miserably short in Noah's shadow. Where does that leave me? Alone and longing for someone I haven't seen in half a decade. Pining away for someone who wants nothing to do with me, who blames me for his sister's death. And searching for a lost brother who doesn't want to be found.

I know they're out there, somewhere. Why hasn't Matty been looking for me? Has Noah moved on? Who am I kidding? It's been years. Of course he has. He could be married with kids by now.

The thought physically hurts me. Another woman living my happily ever after.

I'm on a never-ending roller coaster, wavering between anger and sadness. I'm tired of feeling lost at sea, wanting desperately to be found.

AFTER BEX'S PERSISTENCE—AND SEVERAL MARTINIS—I finally relent and give my number to Christopher.

He isn't exactly boyfriend material, but I figure if I'm to start dating, I need to be able to spend an evening in a man's company.

So here I am, Friday night, getting ready for my date. I feel like I should be excited and obsessing over what to wear, but I honestly don't care if he likes my outfit or thinks I'm pretty. I'm simply going through the motions because this is what normal people are supposed to do.

I put on black skinny jeans, a flowing white top with blue embroidery that Bex says makes me look elegant but not sexy, and some blue Chucks, because date or no date, I'm not wearing heels. I've never really gotten the hang of them; I guess I prefer my feet planted firmly on the ground. I glance at the clock. He'll be here in ten minutes, so I slap on some mascara and lip gloss, then head downstairs to have a glass of wine to calm my nerves and combat my urge to cancel this farce.

Glass in hand, I sit in the living room, waiting for this night to be over when it hasn't even begun yet. Why can't I move on? Why can't I fall in love with someone else? Am I destined to spend the rest of my life alone, waiting for a guy I loved when I was sixteen?

Christopher knocks on my door twenty minutes

late. Strike one. I can't handle people being late; it's a sign of disrespect in my eyes. I contemplate pretending I'm not home but reconsider. It won't kill me to go on one date a year, and maybe he has a legitimate reason for being late.

When I open the door, he's staring down at his phone, texting. He doesn't glance up until I clear my throat.

"You ready?" is all he says before turning his back to me and walking toward his car. No compliments or friendly banter, nothing.

I stare at his back in annoyed disbelief for a few seconds before sighing and locking up. It seems his charming act is just for blushing coeds, because the version I'm getting is kind of a dick. I open my own door and climb into his car.

"Where we headed?" I ask with a smile, determined to put a positive spin on tonight.

"Dulcie's on Sixth."

"Oh, I heard that place is good."

The waitress leads us through the busy restaurant, Christopher's eyes attached to her ass as it sways through the maze of tables. I follow him, texting Bex about what an asshat he's being already.

Once seated, we order wine and peruse the

menu. After a few minutes, the waitress comes to take our order.

"She'll have the kale salad, and I'll have the T-bone with a side salad."

He ordered me a salad. A freaking *salad*.

"*She* will have the mushroom burger with fries, thank you," I say, handing her my menu. Her eyes are wide at the mini-scene developing, and I can almost guarantee she'll be telling her friends about the douche who tried to make his date eat a salad.

He rolls his eyes once the waitress walks away. "I assumed you were on a diet. Most chicks are—no offense."

"Whatever, Christopher. Could you act like something resembling a gentleman for five minutes before I kick your ass?"

He smirks and shakes his head. "I'll try."

We manage a little awkward small talk until our food is delivered. I for one am happy for the excuse to stop talking. The meal is delicious, and I devour every crumb, much to my date's dismay. When the waitress comes to collect our plates, she asks if we'd like dessert.

"No, I'll be licking dessert off her later."

I tell her no and shoot a scowl at him, already regretting this date. "That's not happening."

He smirks. "Playing hard to get? I'm used to a different kind of date, but I'm up for a challenge."

"Whatever. I don't want to spend my evening arguing with you, as much fun as this has been." I need to change the subject before I smack him. "My show is this weekend if you want to stop by. I think it's some of my best work."

"That's cute. Maybe you'll sell a few, make enough to keep snapping your little weddings as your day job."

The elitist douche has some nerve to look down on me and my work.

"I do quite well 'snapping weddings,' actually. My calendar is booked solid for the next two months." Why do I feel the need to defend myself to him?

"Yeah, but it's not like you're creating art. It's just filling a void."

I try to calm my murderous rage before speaking. "Isn't that your specialty? Filling young coeds' voids, telling them all kinds of sweet things to get them in front of your camera?"

He scoffs. "I knew this would end up being some petty revenge plot."

"Revenge plot? I thought this was a date. Clearly that was an illusion, or maybe I'm a grown-up now and you prefer girls who can't think for themselves."

"A date?" He laughs. "I don't *date*. I fuck beautifully, and I create incomparable art."

"Do you even hear yourself talk? You're such a douchebag. I can't believe I asked you out." I down the rest of my drink in one gulp. "My work might not be selling out shows at the Guggenheim, but I'm proud of who I am and how far I've come. I grew up with nothing, and when my mother walked out on me, I could have slipped through the cracks, but I didn't. I made something of myself."

"I imagine it was difficult growing up with a mother like that. Though, I suppose it's lucky she left when she did. You managed to make something of yourself even though you were born into a legacy of white trash."

I stand up so fast the chair shoots out behind me and falls over. "This was a mistake," I state before leaving. Once outside, I lean against the building, wiping away angry tears with the back of my hand, trying to understand why the hell I thought dating was the answer to my problems.

Christopher walks outside, lighting a cigarette before he looks at me. "Your place or mine?"

I stand there fuming, staring at him. He can't seriously expect to get lucky after this. Does he really think I'm that kind of girl?

Funny thing is, once upon a time, I might have. Maybe when I was younger and starved of love and attention, I would have fallen into his bed. I would have pretended he cared for me while he used my body for the night. But Noah showed me what love really is. Because of him, I'll never fall for a fake version of what we had.

"Neither, thanks. I'm going home, alone."

Looking confused, he shakes his head before saying, "Fine, whatever. I'll drive you home." When I take a minute to answer, he speaks up again. "Relax. It's pretty obvious this wasn't a good idea. Just get in the damn car. I'm not going to leave you here alone."

With a shrug, I climb in his car and buckle up. The ride to my place is quiet and loaded with tension. When we pull up outside my house, I try to open my door, but it's locked. My stomach drops as I cling to the door handle.

"What the hell was this, Alexa? You asked me out. You flirt with me every time I come into the club. I thought you were finally ready to hook up, not continue to be a fucking tease," he spits before I feel his cold, rough hand grab my thigh. I try to pry it off, but his fingers dig in painfully. "No one says no to me. You want to play games? Let's play."

He forces his hand between my legs, and instinct takes over almost immediately.

I grab his pinky and bend it back until I hear a crack. Christopher screams a curse that echoes through the small space. Knowing that won't stop him, I swing my elbow back with as much force as I can muster into his nose. Another satisfying crack signals my time to exit. While he hunches over, holding his bleeding nose, I reach over him and hit the Unlock button before fleeing. I run up the stairs, grabbing my keys from my purse.

Just as I slide the key into the lock, I hear a door slam behind me. "You broke my nose, you fucking bitch!"

"And your finger. Now go home before I call the cops," I warn.

That doesn't stop him. He continues to amble toward me. I get the door open, slamming it behind me and locking the door. I grab my cell out of my purse with a shaky hand and dial 911, telling the dispatcher my address over Christopher's banging and cursing at the door.

"You think you can treat me like this, you stupid white trash bitch? You aren't worth the money I spent on dinner."

From inside I can hear a police siren approaching, followed by the sound of his car starting and squealing off into the night.

I collapse on the floor, crying, until the police officer knocks on the door. I spend the next hour answering questions and making a statement. The officer strongly suggests filing a restraining order. Just the way you want a date to end, with broken bones and a visit from the police.

Dating officially sucks, and I'm going to die alone with fifty cats.

Bex went to dinner with her boyfriend, Craig, tonight, so she missed all the chaos but walked through the door in a panic after seeing a police car in the driveway. "What happened?"

"Christopher happened. He jumped me after our date."

"Holy shit! Are you okay?"

"Yeah, just a bit bruised. I broke his finger and nose though. Hopefully he'll think twice before forcing himself on another woman," I say with a smile.

"You're amazing! I'm so proud of you."

"That should be everything, Miss Raine, but don't hesitate to call us if he comes back. And think about that restraining order," the officer says, putting his notebook away.

"I will. Thank you." I walk him out.

When I come back in, Bex is in the kitchen making tea. I sit at the counter, staring down at my favorite pair of Chucks that are now stained with the blood of a douchebag. How did my day go so wrong?

"You gonna be okay?" she asks.

"Yeah. I mean, it was awful, but I feel empowered, and for the first time in a long time, I don't feel like a victim. I saved myself."

"Hell yeah you did." She grinned.

"How was your date with Craig?"

"Good, I guess. I don't know. I really like him, but I feel like he's not in it 100 percent, you know?"

Craig was our ex-manager at Shots, and he was a nice guy, kind and attentive to Bex. "Maybe it was an off night for him."

"Maybe. I'm dead on my feet. Night, Lex," she says, pulling me into a hug.

"Night."

I sit up for another hour searching social media before I head to bed. Curled into myself, I let the tears flow freely. Here in the dark, I can shed my secret tears.

I wish Matty was here. He would be so proud of me. My heart aches thinking about him, wondering where he could be right this minute. Does he have a wife or children to keep safe and kiss goodnight? Or is he alone like me?

I want to believe he's happy. Same with Noah. I hope he's living a life that makes him happy. Maybe they left me because they didn't love me as much as I loved them. I try so hard to ignore the voices that convince me to believe the worst about myself. Did they choose to leave me and to stay gone?

I break down when I look at the butterflies. No matter what I accomplish in my life or how many years pass, the ache of the missing pieces of my soul makes me feel like I'll never be whole again.

Most days I can pretend I'm okay. That this life I've made for myself is enough. My career, my friends are enough. I'm not ungrateful for what I have. I love Bex and my work, and Lana and John have given me a life full of love and a future. But with Matty still missing and Noah's disappearance from my life, I feel the cold emptiness they left in their wake tonight.

Running my finger over my butterfly tattoos that have become a full sleeve, I send a silent prayer to my best friend. Elise's love is still saving me, even from heaven. "I miss you. Please, Elise, help me find them."

What Noah and I shared was one drop of water in the sea of my life. I tell myself it wasn't as perfect as I remember. That I was a lonely kid from a loveless home, and the love and attention he showed me was seen through rose-colored glasses. I try and fail to convince myself that our love wasn't magical. In the dark, I cling to those moments we shared, when love was pure and my heart was full and the whole world stood at our feet.

I fall asleep staring at the picture of us I've kept beside my bed all these years, knowing what I tell myself is all lies. He was the magic in my life, and our love was the real deal. I've felt empty every day since we parted.

MY SHOW OPENS WITH HUGE SUCCESS, AND ALL MY photos sell. The night is a whirlwind of schmoozing with strangers and trying to accept praise gracefully, which is not something I manage very well. Insults I can take like a pro, but compliments have a harder time penetrating my protective shell.

Christopher shows up toward the end of the night. He offers an apology, but I'm not interested.

"Leave now before I call the cops again. You came to say sorry? Fine, you did that. Now please leave." If there is one thing my childhood taught me, it was how to spot an abuser, and that's the last thing I need in my life. Thankfully he leaves without any drama or issue.

By the time the show is over, my introvert self is ready to climb into bed and recharge for a week.

"Brilliant night. Congrats, Lexi," Sarah says, her fiancé, Derrick, beside her, both here to support me.

"Thank you for coming. I'll see you guys next week so you can see the proofs from your shoot before your mom gets them." We all have a laugh at the expense of her overbearing mother and say our goodbyes. It was a wonderful night, and after the dust settles, I'm so proud of myself—another sold-out show.

SITTING AT THE BREAKFAST TABLE THE NEXT DAY, I'M sipping my coffee and scrolling through Instagram, as one does, when Bex runs in the room, squealing, "They wrote an article about your show!"

"What? Who did?"

"The local newspaper. Look," she says, laying the paper flat on the table and tapping the page. "Alexa Raine Photography shows promise. Her raw and whimsical photos are going to take the art world by storm."

My whole body tingles with excitement. "Oh my God" is all I can muster. Pride overwhelms me. I've never felt like anyone cared what I was doing. I didn't dare hope for this kind of reaction.

"I'm so proud of you, Lexi," she says, giving me a hug.

"I couldn't have done any of this without you." I wipe the tears flooding my eyes. I'm so damn proud of myself.

THIRTEEN

I'M IN THE EARLY PLANNING STAGES FOR A NEW SHOW about skin art and its healing properties. I love tattoos, always have. I sport a full sleeve on my left arm, incorporating vines and flowers around the swarm of butterflies, one for each person who loved me. Lana, John, and Bex's butterflies were added to the mix over the years.

In addition to my full sleeve, I have a camera tattooed on my right forearm; I got that one my first year of college. And behind my right ear are the words *For you I shall live*, for Elise. On my hip, I have *I'll carry you with me, until we meet again.* And on the ring finger of my left hand, I have a crown, immortalizing Noah King forever. In my heart, I'll always be married to him; no other man measures up. After five years, they're still a part of who I am.

"Morning," Bex greets me. "I've booked us with the best tattooists the city has to offer. We'll split the meetings." She hands me a piece of paper with three tattoo parlors listed and appointment times beside them. "Here's your share,"

"Whoever manages to make it home without a new tattoo wins," I say with a smile. We're both slightly addicted to ink, and the fact that we'll be spending the whole day in tattoo shops means one or both of us will probably cave.

Bex laughs. "You're on."

"Take pictures of anything that looks like it might be a good candidate. I'm looking for truly remarkable stories that go with their ink. The theme is 'Our bodies are the canvases for our life stories. What does yours say?' Or something like that."

"You got it, boss. Ugh, life is hard. I have to hang out with hot tattoo artists all day." She gathers her list and phone, shoving them into her massive purse. "I'm off. My first shop opens in twenty. See you for supper. It's your turn to order in."

Though we do know how to cook, I confess we get takeout more than we should.

My first stop is Quicksilver Ink. It's a relatively

small shop. When I walk in, I'm greeted by a young girl with purple hair and seven facial piercings. Seven. I'm no prude, but all I can think of is them getting snagged in my hair or something equally horrifying and ripping one out.

"Hi, I'm Alexa Raine. I have an appointment with the manager at ten thirty."

"Okay, she's waiting in her office through there. Last door on the left," she says, pointing down a hallway.

I thank her and make my way toward the office.

Seraphina, the owner, looks like a fifties pinup, and I immediately love her style. She's kind and seems very interested in what I'm trying to do with my show. As luck would have it, one of her clients who would be a perfect fit is scheduled to stop by this morning. She shows me her portfolio as well as the books for the two other artists who work there.

The perfect fit Seraphina mentioned is Joseph, a marine whose body is a rich tapestry of his life and trials in the military. We spend an hour talking about his life before, during, and after his service. Losing friends. Something we have in common, to watch someone close to you die, in your arms. Watching the life drain out of them. We shed a few tears, and he agrees to pose for me. We set up a time for him to stop by the studio and say our goodbyes.

At my next stop, I find a few pictures in their portfolio of a breast cancer survivor who has intricate tattoos covering her double mastectomy scars. I know the moment I see her picture that she's my next subject. I can only hope she agrees to it. The shop can't give me her information, but I leave mine and they promise to contact her and relay the information.

Other people's stories and struggles move me, their pain, how they keep moving forward in their lives when all else seems hopeless. This show means more to me than any other, and I even consider being a subject myself. Show my scars and how my ink saved my life more times than I can count. It's all I've got to remember the important people in my life.

The next shop doesn't specialize in the kind of tattoos I'm looking for, so I leave my card behind for any future clients they think might be interested in sharing their story. They don't have any leads for me, but they do refer me to another tattoo shop, King of Hearts. The owner is rumored to do great work and specializes in the type of tattoos I'm looking for. Once I get to my car, I call and try to get in to see them today. No luck—they're too slammed today to see me, so I book an appointment for later in the week.

Exhausted and ready to call it a day, I pick up a pizza and head home. Bex arrives shortly after me, so we sit down to compare stories and pictures of possible clients.

Without saying a word, Bex slides a twenty over the table, and I immediately start laughing. "You caved?" She shows me a sweet little tattoo of an antique key she got on her wrist. "How cute was the artist?" I know my sister, and hot tattoo artists are her kryptonite.

"Ugh, so freaking cute it physically hurt talking to him," she says, falling back on the couch.

I can't help but laugh. "Did you get his number?"

"No, he was wearing a wedding ring. I told him if he ever gets divorced to call me."

"You didn't!"

"Oh yes I did. He was flattered, but the receptionist wasn't. Apparently she's his wife."

"Bex! Could you not sully my business name with your whorish ways?"

"It's fine! I apologized and told her she was lucky to find a good one. We were besties by the time I left."

. . .

BEX AND I HEAD TO SHOTS A BIT EARLY. SHE WANTS to rub up on her boyfriend before he opens the bar since she hasn't seen him all week.

"You're not going to have sex with him in his office while I'm sitting at the bar, are you?"

She looks at me with wide, fake-innocent eyes, like I haven't had to endure their grunting and groaning every other time we go to the bar early. "I would never!"

"Yeah right, pervert."

We both laugh our way into the bar.

The minute we walk in, he comes into view: Craig, Bex's latest jerkface boyfriend, with his hands on the new waitress's ass, pressed against the bar with his tongue down her throat. I watch Bex to gauge her reaction, and I can see shit's about to get real.

"You low-down dirty motherfucker," Bex mutters before she launches herself at them, screaming like a banshee.

"Oh shit." I run after her, trying to stop this from turning into an episode of *Jerry Springer*.

The girl screams when Bex pulls her away from Craig by the hair.

He raises his hands, pleading, "Becca, babe, it's nothing. She got a little friendly, but that's all it was, honest."

"Bullshit. We've had sex in his office every day this week. Whatever, I quit," the girl whines before she tosses her apron on the floor and walks out.

"You're a pig," I shout at him before turning to guide Bex out the door. Why does she keep giving her whole heart to these losers?

She breaks down when we get in the car.

"You're smart, beautiful, and worthy of so much more than the likes of him. Craig's a giant asshat and deserves to have his cock rot off." This gets a smile.

"I should be more like you, Lex. Not put myself out there to be hurt."

Her words are like a blow to the heart. Have I really closed myself off? Am I leading a coward's life by refusing to put myself out there? "We both could benefit from acting a bit like each other. You're too open, and I'm way too closed off."

"Together we're the perfect person."

We smile at each other sadly, then laugh.

A FEW DAYS LATER, I WALK THROUGH THE DOOR OF King of Hearts Tattoo and Piercing, shaking the rain off my umbrella when I'm confronted with a frazzled-looking woman running around the reception desk.

"Are you all right?" I ask.

"Have you seen a pain-in-the-ass, bratty kid hiding around here?"

"A kid? No." I'm a bit startled by her aggression toward a child and also wondering why there's a kid hanging out in a tattoo parlor.

"You're from Alexa Raine Photography, right? The two o'clock consult?"

"Yes, ma'am."

"Well, you're early, and he's not finished yet. I've got a brat to find because apparently on-call babysitter is in my freaking job description. Take a seat. You can browse some of their books while you wait."

I nod in response. She's kind of rude for a receptionist, but it looks like she's having a rough day, so I let it slide. I settle in and begin flipping through pages of some seriously impressive work.

I hear a delicate sneeze coming from somewhere behind me. I peek over the back of the couch and spot a little girl with blonde ringlets and big blue eyes looking up at me. "Marco!" she yells. I watch her curiously.

From somewhere in the back room, I hear the receptionist grumble, "Dammit, Jess, I don't have time to play that stupid game with you."

I turn toward the little girl and whisper, "Polo," before turning back to the book I was flipping through. Her melodic giggle puts a smile on my face. Brat, my ass, she's obviously adorable.

She crawls out, standing in front of me with wide eyes, her mouth forming a tiny circle. "Are you a princess? You look just like the princess. Are you getting a tattoo? I like your butterflies." She reaches out, tracing the butterflies and flowers decorating my forearm. This girl is so stinking sweet.

"Thank you. No, I'm not a princess, but you certainly look like one," I reply, motioning to the flowing pink dress she has on. "Why are you hiding from your mom?"

Her precious face scrunches up in disgust. "She's not my mom! That's *Anabelle*." She hisses the name like it's a disease, looking in the direction the rude woman went. "She answers the phone and stuff for Daddy, but she's mean. She never has candy and never wants to play with me." The whole time she's talking, she's touching my face. Is it normal for a child to touch your face? Because it feels weird. "You really are the princess!"

"I'm not—"

"Daddy!" she yells, inches from my face, before running off behind the counter somewhere. I guess that explains why she's here: her dad owns the place.

The girl returns a minute later dragging behind her who I can only assume is her daddy. He's tall with shaggy dark blond hair and an impressive beard. "Daddy, you *have* to see her. She's the princess, the one from Uncle Noah's tattoo."

My heart stops beating, and it feels like the world freezes as I stare at this sweet little girl standing next to her daddy—Marco. We stand frozen, staring for what feels like a lifetime, our eyes locked on each other. Tears well up, ready to overflow, and I can't stop staring.

Is this real?

"Marco?"

"Holy shit, Lexi?" He charges at me, sweeping me up in a hug, and we both start crying.

I lean back, looking at his face. I push back his shaggy hair and see the tattoo I gave him over his eye.

"It's really you." I bury my face in his chest.

"Daddy?" Jess looks confused watching our interaction.

Marco gets down on one knee in front of her and says, "Sweetheart, this is Miss Lexi. She was your mama's best friend while you were in her tummy."

I can't help the sob that erupts from my chest. I drop to my knees and stare at her sweet face; I see Elise and Marco mixed in her petite features. Blinking back tears, I stare at Marco questioningly. "She survived?"

He nods, and I lose it. I ugly cry loud and completely break down. I want to pick up this sweet baby girl and squish her with everything I have, but I don't want to scare her.

Marco sits down next to me, wrapping his arms around me.

She's alive. I can't even begin to wrap my head around this.

"Don't be sad, Princess Lexi," Jess comforts me, placing her small hand on my cheek. I love her already.

"Can I give you a hug, sweetheart?"

"Of course you can, silly. Hugs always help when you're feeling sad." She holds out her arms, ready to comfort me. This girl, she's a miracle.

"What the hell is going on out here?" someone

says behind me. I stand up as Noah walks in, locking eyes with me. "Lexi?"

This can't be real.

I'm frozen in place with tear-filled eyes. The shock wears off after a few moments of silence, and we run into each other's embrace.

I'm finally home again.

Have I really been given this incredible gift?

"Is this real? I feel like I'm dreaming." I lean back and run my fingers through his hair, over his face, touching as much of him as I can to convince myself he's really standing here.

A throat clearing behind Noah draws our attention. Anabelle stands, looking pissed and shocked at the scene in front of her. Noah pulls away from me, looking guilty.

She's staring at Noah with tears in her eyes. I wait for him to introduce me, but he stands stoic, lost in thought.

I can't stand here awkwardly anymore, so I offer a smile, deciding to break the ice. "Sorry for the excitement, I haven't seen these guys in years. I wasn't sure if I'd ever.... Anyway, I'm Lexi Raine." I hold my hand out.

Her eyes widen at the sound of my name. *"You're* Lexi?"

"Alexa Raine?" Noah asks.

"I was adopted by my aunt."

"You're Lexi?" Anabelle asks again, this time looking at Noah for confirmation.

I turn to Noah, waiting for him to respond, but he's staring at Marco. Having no idea what's happening, I shrug, smiling at her. "That's me. Nice to meet you."

She reaches for my hand. "I'm Anabelle, Noah's girlfriend."

And the floor drops out from beneath me. All sound dissolves as those words settle over my soul. *Girlfriend*. It's too late.

"Oh" is all I can muster. Before dropping her hand, I look to Marco. "Sorry, I actually have to reschedule… our meeting. I have an, um… appointment I forgot about. I've… got to go."

I can't be here. I need to leave. I'm going to break down at any second, and I can't be here when that happens. Fight-or-flight kicks in, and I turn and walk out without saying another word. I run out so fast I forget my coat, and by the time I get to my car, the rain has soaked me to the bone. Noah's voice is yelling after me, but all I hear are the words *"Noah's girlfriend."*

Once I'm safely inside my car, I let loose years of

anger and frustration, beating my fists against the steering wheel, screaming. I've lived here for four years and he was here the whole time. I feel like an idiot for running out, but there was no way I could stand there and pretend everything I ever wanted was right in front of me and still out of reach. I can't watch him with someone else.

A tap on the window startles me. Noah is standing beside my car.

"Open the door, Lex... please." I shake my head. "I'll break it if you don't open the door. I won't let any obstacle come between us again, not even this goddamn window."

Unable to deny him anything, I open the door. I continue to cry as he pulls me from the car out into the rain. I want him to hold me so bad I can't breathe, but I keep my distance. He isn't mine anymore, and that fact makes me furious.

"That girl in there is a pretty big freaking obstacle, Noah. God, I'm such an idiot. I missed you so much. I can't do this. I waited for you! I knew you hated me, but like an idiot, I still waited for you to one day forgive me," I scream at him, hitting his chest.

"Hate you? How could I ever hate you? I'm sorry I hurt you."

"It was all for nothing. All those years of me loving you, waiting for you, and you were loving someone else. I can't do this, Noah. I can't listen to you tell me how wonderful she is. I don't care. I'm sorry, but I don't want to hear it. If that makes me a selfish bitch, fine. I can't…. Please let me go!" As I sob uncontrollably, I get back into my car, but he keeps hold of the door, refusing to let me leave. I'm in no shape to drive, and he sees that.

"I just found you. I won't lose you again, dammit! You can't drive in this condition. Please, Lexi love, let me help you get home."

At the sound of his name for me, I close my eyes and my head falls against the headrest, my heart cracking wide open. I shake my head. "No, this needs to be over now." I need to cut him out of my life once and for all.

"This is not fucking over," he yells.

"Enough." Marco pushes past Noah, takes my hand, and guides me out of the driver seat to the other side. He sits me down and buckles my belt like I'm a child. I'm grateful, as I don't think I could have managed on my own. I'm in shock, unable to stop replaying everything over and over in my head. What just happened? I was given everything and had it ripped away before I had a moment to enjoy it.

Noah stands stoic in the rain, watching as I stare at him with wide, tear-filled eyes, my whole body shaking. Marco tosses him a set of keys. "Follow us."

Marco gets behind the wheel, asking, "Address?"

I manage to mumble it to him; my voice is croaky and barely recognizable. The car starts moving and still I stare at Noah. He stares back as he walks toward a truck in the parking lot.

His face is rougher than I remember. Of course, he was a boy then. He's a man now, with hard edges; he survived his sister's death, after all, and that changes a person. The boy I loved is gone forever. Lost in one night of gunfire and heartbreak. Our whole world was ripped to shreds, and every day I prayed he would find me, he wasn't even looking. He was with her, falling in love with her. I close my eyes tight, trying to block the images of him with her.

"Are you okay?" Marco asks.

"No, Marco. I don't think I am." I try smiling to reassure him, but the tremble in my chin gives away my heartbreak. Hopeless tears fall down my cheeks and onto my hands clenched in my lap.

This is irrational. I can't be heartbroken. He isn't even mine. He hasn't been mine for a long time. I try to talk myself down, take deep breaths, but my heart whispers, *He'll always be mine.*

"Babe." Noah's voice startles me. He's standing outside the open car door with his hand out.

I look around, confused. The rain has stopped, and we're at my house. When did we get here?

Taking his hand, I gasp at the contact but allow him to help me out of the car. My whole body shivers violently, though from the rain-soaked clothes or the presence of Noah, it's a toss-up.

"You're really here?" He smiles sadly, touching my cheek, gently wiping the tears away. I lean into his touch, inhaling his scent. "Lexi, I thought I'd never see you again. Where have you been? Please, can we talk? I can't leave you right now. Please don't make me leave."

I nod, turning toward the house.

Once I get to the door, Bex opens it before I get my keys. Seeing my face and the two heavily tattooed and equally soaked men with me, she goes on high alert. "What the hell happened? Are you okay?" I wipe a tear off my cheek and shake my head. Her gaze shifts between me, Noah, and then Marco. "What is going on?"

"Bex, this is Noah and Marco. Guys, this is my sister Rebekah."

She gasps, covering her mouth. "Holy shit. Noah?"

He shrugs. "In the flesh."

"Lexi, why aren't you ecstatic right now? This is amazing!" Seeing I am in fact not ecstatic, she frowns. "Are you okay?"

"No, and I really wish everyone would stop asking me that!" I yell as I grab three towels out of the bathroom, tossing one to each of the guys.

Noah comes to stand in front of me, so close. I lift my hand to touch him, then shake my head and pull my hand back before it makes contact.

"We need to talk," he whispers.

I'm afraid anything I say or do will burst this bubble and I'll wake up from this dream, so I simply nod, letting him take my hand. Leading him to my room and closing the door behind us, I sit on the bed before my legs give out, and he stands by the door, watching me.

For a moment, we stare at each other, both willing our minds to believe this is happening. Then Noah collapses on his knees in front of me. He rests his head against my lap and cries. Anguished, painful cries that rip my soul in two. We cling to each other.

"I'm sorry. I should have listened. I should never have gone back there. I'm so sorry." I'm holding on to him so tight I don't ever want to let go again. I'll live in this moment for as long as we can. I know it'll be over in the blink of an eye. He'll go back to his girlfriend and his life will keep rushing forward without me, but this moment belongs to us.

"No, it was my fault. I should have gotten there sooner. I should have fought harder to see you at the hospital. Should have come for you when they released me from jail. When I was released my mom was there. She was inconsolable and she took Jess from the hospital saying the child was in danger. Given the circumstances of her birth they allowed temporary custody. After Elise… we were all broken. Our whole family was torn apart. I'm so sorry, Lexi." His lips brush over mine. "I never stopped loving you."

I pull him to me, unable to stand the space between us for another second. My whole body aches with need for him. Our lips speak our love and desperation with every touch. I wrap my legs around him, and we fall back on the bed. I need more of him. Five long years and I've found the other half of my soul. I'll fight for him, for us. Nothing will take him away from me again.

Noah's cell phone rings in his pocket. "Shit," he whispers before he kisses me one last time, slowly.

Fate is a bitch.

FOURTEEN

Noah's cell rings again, breaking the spell we're under. He glances down, the name "Anabelle" flashing across it. It kills me, but the love of my life pulls away and stands up.

"You should go, Noah. This has to be really confusing for her."

"She knows about you."

I stare at him in shock. "Why would you tell her about me?"

He pulls his shirt over his head. There, on his chest, sits a stunning sketch of my face, tattooed on his skin. It looks real. I reach out, running my fingers over the lines of my face and the letters of my name. "I had to tell her, to explain this."

What did he tell her? Why did he get this to remember me?

"Why?"

"Because I love you, Lexi. It's always been you. I carried you with me every single day we were apart." He runs his finger over the crown tattooed on my finger. "Looks like you carried a piece of me with you too."

"I called, but you didn't want anything to do with me."

"What? I would never say that."

"Your mother, she told me you hated me for what happened to Elise, that you never wanted to see me again."

"God, Lexi, I had no idea. I'm so sorry she said that to you. My mom went crazy after Elise died. She took Jess and me back home with her. I was such a wreck. She blocked Marco from seeing Jess and tried to get custody. It was a mess. Luckily, the judge saw through her bullshit. When Marco came to pick up Jess, I left with him. I haven't seen or spoken to her in years. I'm so sorry." He pulls me into a hug, kissing my forehead.

"We can't do this, Noah. Please, I need time to process this. You have a girlfriend."

Leaning in, he brushes his lips against mine. His cell goes off again.

With a sigh, I put some distance between us. "You should go to her, Noah. This isn't right. She doesn't deserve this."

Bex and Marco are standing in the kitchen making awkward small talk when we return. I walk over and hug Marco. "I need to see you and Jess again, soon," I say, writing my number down on a piece of paper and handing it to him.

"You bet. I'll call you," he says, hugging me again before whispering in my ear, "Give him a chance, Lex. Life doesn't just hand out miracles like this every day."

I nod, trying to stop the tears from falling.

We say our goodbyes, and Noah pulls me into his arms. "Don't give up on me, Lexi love."

My heart melts at his name for me. I've loved him with my whole heart for so long. Before pulling away, I whisper, "Never." I'll fight for him until my last breath.

Once they leave, it takes Bex about three seconds to freak out. "What the hell just happened? Where did you find him? Why aren't you jumping up and down excited right now? Why did he leave and take that fine-ass man with him?"

She always knows how to make me laugh, even when I want to cry.

"Lord, where do I even start? I found him at King of Hearts, owned by Noah King and Marco Heart. I'm not freaking happy because two seconds after I found him, I also came face-to-face with his girl-friend." I collapse onto the couch and cover my face with a pillow. "I totally freaked out, Bex. I stammered and basically ran out of there. Marco had to drive me home because I was catatonic. It was so humiliating."

"He has a girlfriend?" I nod in response, the pillow movement her only clue at my reply. "Lexi, do you for two seconds think that that man doesn't love you? That he isn't about to dump this girl so fast her head's going to spin? He's probably doing it right now." She takes the pillow off my face. "Alexa Raine, you have nothing to worry about. He will come running back to you a single pringle, ready to mingle."

"But that poor girl—"

"Fuck that girl." When I try to interrupt her, she pushes on. "This is *your* happily ever after, not hers. Trust me, she knows this. It sucks for her, no doubt about it, but I won't let you miss out on this because you're worried about hurting her feelings."

"You're right, as usual." I take a deep breath. "She's alive, Bex."

"Who's alive?"

"Elise and Marco's baby. She survived the shooting. You've got to meet her. She's a miracle, that girl. So sweet and bossy, like her mom." I start tearing up again. "She's so beautiful."

Bex pulls me into a hug. "I'm so happy for you, Lex. This is a miracle. You can't throw that away."

"That's what Marco said."

She smirks. "Damn, he's so freaking sexy my panties dissolved when our eyes locked. *Dissolved*. And when he spoke… oh Lord. I seriously had to hold myself back. I wanted to lick all his tattoos."

Bursting out laughing, I smack at her. "Oh my God, you're such a pervert. I was in there having a moment and you were out here trying not to lick my friend."

She just shrugs and starts making tea.

"When will you see Noah again?" she asks after a moment.

"I don't know. Soon, I hope."

I MEET UP WITH MARCO AND JESS A COUPLE DAYS later at their place for brunch. Jess and I had such a strange first meeting, and I wanted to spend more time with her and get a chance to get to know her without Noah as a distraction.

"Princess Lexi!" I turn to see sweet Jess running to me excitedly. *Well, so much for breaking the ice slowly.* I kneel and catch her as she barrels into me.

"Hello there, sweetheart. It's so good to see you again. You look super cute today." She's wearing the smallest Joan Jett T-shirt I've ever seen, paired with a pink tutu and green shoes with butterflies on her feet.

"Thank you. I picked it out special for you. See, butterflies!" She points at her shoes.

"Those are so pretty! I wish I had shoes like those." I place her back on the ground and turn to her father, giving him a quick hug. "You look good, Marco. What's with all the fuzz?" I say, pointing to his beard. "You're like a lumberjack."

"You like? It's a chick magnet."

"Ew. TMI, Marco." Though I don't doubt it. He's a handsome man and clearly a great father.

"Seriously, women take one peek at my tattoos and my manly beard and they flock to me." He laughs.

"Sexy, tattooed lumberjack single dad. Yup, that's like crack to women."

"Wanna touch it?" he says, scratching his beard.

I laugh, shaking my head. "No! Who knows where that thing has been? Look at you though. You're such a great daddy."

Marco brings out Jess's baby pictures, and we are both getting overemotional over beautiful memories. We sit there on his deck, watching Jess make and chase bubbles all over the back yard. "I thought she had died with Elise. I can't believe she made it. She's such a miracle, Marco," I say as we continue flipping through pictures.

"I know. She had a rough start to life. First fighting to survive while her mom died, then fighting to stay with me. It was a battle getting her away from her grandmother. I wasn't sure any judge would give me custody with the way I look. It was like Elise was with me that day in court."

I pull out the book of pictures I've kept all these years. "I brought you something. I wasn't sure if I should, but I figured you and Jess might like it." I pass the photo album to him. "These pictures kept me going when I felt like I was falling apart."

He gasps when he opens the book, stopping when he gets to one of Elise. It's my favorite picture of her. We're at the beach, the sun making her golden hair glow like a halo. She was so beautiful. "She was always an angel. Her heart was open, and she loved so fully. She really was perfect, wasn't she? Some days I think it was all in my head, that she seemed so perfect because she was taken from me too soon. But she was. I didn't deserve her. This whole world didn't deserve her light." Tears flow from his eyes as he stares at his lost love.

"She's saved me quite a few times since she died. Just the memory of her friendship and love saved me," I say, touching the butterfly tattoo. "I'm so sorry, Marco. I should never have gone back to the apartment that day. I should have listened. I'm sorry." I start to sob.

He pulls me into a hug. "It's wasn't your fault, Lexi. Life isn't fair. That is one of the hardest lessons I've had to learn. When she died, I was in a bad place. I wanted to curl up beside her and die. But she wouldn't have it. She left me this miracle, this piece of her. I couldn't wallow in my grief too long. I needed to be the father I promised Elise I'd be."

Jess runs up to us holding her shoe. "Daddy, can you untie this big old knot? It's too tricky for me."

"Of course, sweetheart," he says, pulling her into

his lap and showing her how to untie it for next time.

"Elise would be so proud of you," I say, and he looks up from her and smiles.

"I don't know about that. I give in to her more than I should. Hasn't been easy. I had to fight Elise's mom for custody, which got messy real fast. If it weren't for Noah, I don't know what I would have done."

"I think you're doing an amazing job. I'm so proud of you. I know it sounds silly, but it's the truth. You were so young and completely on your own."

"I had Noah." My smile drops at the mention of his name. "Lexi, it's not serious, what he has with her. He loves you. Always has, always will."

"She sure seemed to act like it was serious when she came face-to-face with me." I sigh. "Look, I figured he would have moved on by now. I just didn't expect to see it up close. I don't think I'll ever be ready to see him with someone else."

"Have you moved on?" Unable to voice an answer, I just shake my head and keep my eyes on Jess's first birthday pictures. He covers my hand with his, giving it a gentle squeeze. "You both need time to process. Neither of you ever thought you'd see each other again. The truth is, he met a girl, she pursued him, and he caved. She helped him forget his pain for a little while. I can tell you right now he doesn't love her."

"I thought he hated me. All these years I've been pining for him, I thought he hated me."

He shrugs. "What can I say? My mother-in-law is a nasty cow who thrives on killing people's spirit. Why do you think Elise and Noah ran away from her?"

"It never occurred to me that she was lying. I believed her. So many years wasted thinking he hated me, blamed me."

"It's always easier to believe the bad things over the good. You blamed yourself for Elise's death, so when she validated that, you took it for scripture."

I smile at him. "Damn, Marco. When did you get so smart?"

"I have my moments." He grins. "Jess has been hounding me to take her to the park. Want to walk with us?"

"No, you guys go enjoy your Sunday, I've got a shoot in a couple hours I need to get ready for."

"Big-shot photographer, just like you always dreamed. I'm proud of you, Lex. Elise and I decided before she died that you and Noah would be the godparents to our child. You don't have to answer now, but think about it. It would mean a lot to me if you'd accept."

I pull him into a hug, fighting another round of tears from surfacing. "Yes, of course I will! Nothing would make me happier. Thank you. I love you guys. See you next week." I kiss Jess on the head and say goodbye. I can't believe I'm going to be this sweet girl's godmother!

I'm buzzing with excited energy as I head back to the studio to finish up some work before the dreaded shoot with Mrs. Neilson and Sarah.

THE NEXT DAY, I'M IN MY GALLERY SETTING UP FOR A client when I hear the bell on the front door ring. I watch as Anabelle, Noah's girlfriend, peruses the photographs hanging on the walls. *What am I supposed to say to this poor girl?*

I swallow my pride and walk out onto the gallery floor. Without looking at me, she talks to the photograph in front of her. "I've been haunted by the memory of you for a long time."

"I'm sorry," I offer.

She shrugs in response. "I always knew if you ever showed up he would leave me in a heartbeat. I hoped that day would never come, but at least it happened before we got married and had children."

I cringe at the thought of breaking up a happy home. "Anabelle, I never meant for any of this to happen. I'm not interested in taking something that doesn't belong to me. He loves you."

"No he doesn't. But that was nice of you to say. This would be easier if you were a bitch."

"I'll stay away from him. I'll—"

Tears glisten in her eyes when she finally looks at me. "I left him. I just wanted you to know that. It's funny. I've hated you for so long. You've always been in the background of our relationship, keeping him from loving me, but seeing you face-to-face, seeing the way he looked at you? As much as it hurts, I don't blame you. You guys were given a shit hand. I won't be the one to stand in your way now that you've found each other."

"It sounds so stupid, but thank you. I'm sorry for hurting you, Anabelle." I start crying.

"I'm a tough girl. It'll take more than this to break me," she says with a sad smile, wiping away the one tear that escapes. Then she walks out of my gallery, giving me Noah.

She's kind of awesome, and it had to be difficult to let go of the man she loves for me. How could he just let her walk away? Did she mean nothing to him? How long after we were separated did he start dating? How many women has he been with? These are the questions keeping me awake at night and stopping me from reaching out to him.

TWO DAYS.

It took Noah all of two days after Anabelle left him before the first text came.

Noah: Good morning, beautiful. I stare at the text for a good five minutes, typing and retyping the perfect response.

Good morning, beautiful. What the hell am I supposed to say to that? Thank you? It's so casual, like I talk to him every day. Good morning, my ass. I stew over his text all freaking day.

When Bex walks in the door after her shift at the shelter, she glances at my scowling face and my phone clenched in my hand and rolls her eyes. "Have you responded yet?"

"And say what?" I screech in a panicked, high-pitched tone.

"Jesus, Lexi. Stop freaking out. Just say 'Hi, I love you, let's get married and make babies.' I'll do it. Give it to me." She tries to snatch the phone out of my hands, but I laugh and swat her away. "Ovary up. He's in your life, single, and he's trying to connect with you. It's your dream come true. Now stop screwing it up with your weirdness and text him back."

"Okay, jeez. So bossy." I turn my phone on and stare at those three words. I want to tell him I love him, that I want to see him, but anything I think of to say sounds stupid in my head. I put my phone face-down. "I can't deal with this right now, I need to finish going over Sarah's pictures and call a bunch of possible clients for my next project. There are a couple of great possibilities. I need to focus on work right now."

"Whatever you say, boss." Bex leaves me be, knowing there's no rushing me on this.

I work late into the night, and once I stretch and finally check the time, it's past midnight. I yawn and shuffle my way through the house, making sure everything is locked up. After washing my face and brushing my teeth, I snuggle into bed, phone in hand. I lie in the dark, thinking about Noah, wanting to hear his voice, touch his skin. Finally, I text him the only thing I can think of.

Me: I can't believe you texted good morning. What an ass thing to text after all these years. I've

been trying to figure out what an appropriate response to that is.

His reply comes almost immediately. He's awake right now, thinking about me. That thought sends my heart racing.

Noah: And you settled on blind rage? I woke up missing you, so I texted good morning. Last week I couldn't do that.

My heart sinks. He's right.

Feeling brave, I start typing again.

Me: Sometimes, I miss you so much I can't breathe.

The phone starts ringing with a video chat. I squeal, throwing it on the bed. I accept but have the camera facing up. Why? Because I've clearly gone insane.

"Lexi, you there?"

"Why did you video chat me?" I ask incredulously.

His chuckle fills my bedroom, and I watch his face on the screen. Damn, he's so sexy. "Babe, pick up the phone. I've missed seeing your beautiful face."

I smile and pick up my phone. His face lights up, and we sit there in silence just staring at each other and smiling.

"Did you have a good day?" I ask, unsure of what to do with myself on camera.

"Yeah, it was pretty slammed most of the day, and I was on Jess duty tonight."

"I love her. She is such a great kid. What did you guys do?"

We chat for a while about our days, and before I know it, it's two in the morning.

"I need to get some sleep. Can I see you... sometime?"

"Yeah, I've got to take Jess to preschool tomorrow morning. I'll stop by after. That work for you?"

"Perfect. I'll be in the gallery all day. Good night, Noah."

"Good night, Lexi love."

I fall asleep with the biggest smile on my face. Life is good, and I really feel like things are finally coming together. Finding the three of them is a miracle.

I'M ON THE PHONE WITH A POTENTIAL CLIENT WHEN he walks in. He flashes me that breathtaking smile and gives a quick wave when I point to the phone and hold up one finger signaling I need a minute.

While attempting to focus on the client's ideas

and questions, I can't help but watch him. His brown hair is cropped short, and he's wearing a black T-shirt that clings to every curve and contour of his body. I get lost watching his movements and apparently forget about my client. "Oh, sorry, ma'am. Yes, I'm still here."

Hearing this, Noah looks my way, smiling, knowing I was ogling him hard.

I smile back, shaking my head. "I'm booked into next month. How's the twenty-third work for you? Excellent, I'll hold the date. Just let me know if anything changes. Thank you," I say, hanging up the phone.

"This is incredible, Lexi, or should I call you Alexa?"

"I thought Alexa sounded more professional," I say, approaching him like a moth to a flame, my heartbeat racing with each step closer. "My aunt Lana bought this place for Bex and me after graduation so we would always have a place to call home."

"Aunt?"

"Erica's sister." His eyes widen. "I know, I thought the social worker had lost her mind. You should have seen her house. It was like a new-age shop puked all over it. I was horrified, but she became the rock I needed in my life. She helped me to finally stop blaming myself... and hurting myself."

His eyes flash to my arm. He lifts my hand and runs his fingers over the sleeve that now decorates my skin, surrounding his butterflies. "She sounds like a trip."

"She taught me what a family should be. She saved me when all I wanted to do was end it all." His gasp is audible, and instantly I feel bad for saying these things when he's the one who lost his sister. "I'm sorry I went back there that night, Noah. I've relived that night over and over, wishing I had made different choices, wishing I could change the outcome. To save her."

He pulls me into his arms and I'm home. I cling to his shirt, never wanting to let go. "We're all haunted by that day, but there's no changing the past. We need to focus on building a future together. We found each other, against all odds. I don't plan on letting go. What about you? It's been five years. Do you... do you have a man?"

I shake my head. "No."

"Thank fuck for that" is all he says before devouring me. Every nerve ending in my body is humming with happiness. The kiss goes on for a blissful eternity, and when we pull apart, we're out of breath, smiling from ear to ear.

"Maybe you should give me a tour before we get carried away. Don't get me wrong, I'm looking forward to it, but we have a lifetime to catch up, and I want you to show me around your studio. I'll try to keep my hands to myself."

"What fun is that?" I say, taking his hand and leading him through to the back, pointing at the studio. "That's where I take pictures. That's where I process them." I keep leading him into the house, closing the door behind us. I start unbuttoning my shirt, smiling up at him, then nod in the direction of the kitchen. "That's the kitchen." I slip my shirt off, letting it fall to the floor. "That's my office. Are we done with the tour yet, or should I continue? Because all I've been thinking about since you walked in is tasting your skin."

He sweeps me up in his arms. "Fuck, I love you."

FIFTEEN

I'VE PLANNED A DINNER TONIGHT FOR NOAH, MARCO, and Jess to meet Bex, John, and Lana. Lana and John are fresh off their Mediterranean cruise, and neither could believe I found Noah and Marco. My family will be together at last—minus Matty, of course. I've continued to search online for him, but either he changed his name or doesn't want to be found. I've limited myself to Google searches since I couldn't afford that private investigator anymore; I'd paid him enough money already, and he didn't find anything anyway. For all I know, he was cashing my checks and not even looking.

Finding Noah has given me hope that somehow, someway, Matty will find me. I won't give up.

. . .

Dinner is going amazingly, and everyone falls hopelessly in love with Jess, naturally. She's a great kid. I take out my camera, needing to immortalize this brilliant evening filled with love and laughter. I can't stop smiling at everyone together. My heart is so full right now.

Throughout the night, my eyes keep finding Noah's and we share a secret smile, one that says we know how lucky we are to have found each other.

"So, you all ended up here, near the coordinates of your tattoos? That really is divine intervention. Someone up there is keeping watch over you," Lana says with a smile.

We all feel it, even if we don't say, that this was Elise's handiwork, guiding us all on our paths leading back together. I have to agree, it's a miracle.

I raise my glass of wine. "Even from heaven she's bossing us around. For Elise." Everyone echoes, "For Elise," toasting our guardian angel. I send out a silent prayer to her to help me find the last piece of my puzzle: my brother Matty.

As the evening grows long, everyone starts to leave. Marco carries a sleeping Jess out to his car, promising to meet up again in a few days. Bex offers Lana and John a ride home; they're a wee bit tipsy after a few too many glasses of wine. Bex kisses me on the cheek, whispering, "I'll stay over at Lana's tonight."

"You don't have to do that."

She just winks at us. "Good night, sister. Love you."

"Love you too."

When the last person leaves, it's just me and Noah left. I rest my back against the door. He's leaning against the opposite wall, arms crossed over his chest. I smile at him, unsure of what to say now that we're alone. I'm barely resisting the urge to pounce on him.

"I better clean up this mess," I say, walking into the kitchen to finish cleaning the last few glasses and dishes from our night. He brings in a few glasses from the living room, and we move with easy familiarity, brushing shoulders occasionally. A dance of anticipation, of longing. We make easy conversation about life and about our careers. We both followed our dreams here and found each other. What are the odds?

After we load the last dish in the dishwasher and wipe the counters, we stand on opposite sides, watching. Smiling. Delaying pleasure. It's a dangerous dance of anticipation and lust.

He makes the first move, coming to stand in

front of me. He brushes the hair out of my face and places it behind my ear. "I've missed you so much, Lex. I have to keep reminding myself that you're real."

"I missed you every day. I looked for you, but the police wouldn't give me any information. And after the phone call with your mother… I almost gave up, I'm sorry, I should have tried harder. If I had kept trying, maybe…." There was no point in finishing the sentence, no point wasting time with what-ifs.

"We found each other, that's all that matters, and I'm never letting you go, Lexi love."

"Will you stay with me tonight?"

"I'll stay forever if you let me." He takes my hand, leading me upstairs where we spend the night in each other's arms, falling in love all over again.

We both survived so much and, by some miracle, ended up here together. After everything I've endured and survived, to be here in his arms is bliss. Being with him is everything to me. All the struggles were worth the fight to finally have him again.

We move together like beautiful music, like two halves of the same soul, our bodies making promises to never be apart again. Then we talk into the wee hours of the morning, lying sated in each other's arms, my head on his chest beside my tattoo. I run my fingers over each line of ink, new and old, convincing myself with every touch that he's real. Noah tells me his side of that night so long ago, the night our lives were ripped apart.

"When we got back to the loft and you girls weren't there, we knew you'd gone back. I was pissed. We walked over to meet you, but when we got there—" He wipes at his eyes in the dark. "You and Elise were just lying there on the sidewalk in a pool of blood. I held your limp bodies, screaming. Marco was in shock. There was no consoling him. Neither of you were moving, and we thought the worst.

"When a guy came running out of the building carrying a gun, I completely lost it and jumped him. We fought, and the gun went flying, so when the cops arrived, it was chaos. Then the guy tried to run, and they shot him in pursuit. Marco and I had blood on our hands. To the cops, we were all guilty until they got all the facts, and they arrested us. They wouldn't even tell me if you girls had survived." He breaks down crying in my arms. I cradle him, wishing I could heal his heart.

"I woke up in the hospital a few days later, alone, sporting two gunshot wounds. At first, they wouldn't tell me anything until I gave the police my statement. They told me they had you in custody. I told them you were innocent. When they told me Elise was dead, I lost it, and they had to sedate me. Day after day I sat in that bed waiting for Matty, for you, for anyone to come for me. When I was in the group home, I called your cell. After talking to your mom, I was broken and alone. God, I was so lost. I never wanted to admit it to myself but I... I tried to kill myself. I couldn't bear to live another day with the gaping hole in my heart."

"I wish I could have taken your pain away. I was lost too. After Elise died, I didn't know what to do. Jess needed me, Marco needed me. I was hollowed out inside and went with my mother because I knew I was Marco's only shot at getting Jess back. Marco wasn't there to see Jess born or Elise die, and by the time we were cleared of all charges, Mother had already taken Jess. I couldn't let her take away all Marco had left of Elise. I tried to find you, I swear I did. I called the hospital, but they wouldn't tell me anything. When I called the hospital again, they said you'd checked out and that was it. I knew I'd lost you forever."

He tells me stories about Jess as a baby and what it was like being two guys trying to figure out what the hell they were doing in the early days. "You wouldn't believe the judgments we got because of our age, our tattoos, and the fact that Jess didn't have a mother. Most people assumed we were gay, and honestly we didn't care. We had our hands full with Jess and didn't give a shit what anyone else thought.

"I went back to your apartment, hoping Matt was there or I could get some information, but the place was emptied out and locked up. The landlord said you came by once but didn't leave any contact information. Fuck, Lexi. I wanted to find you. The cops wouldn't tell us anything about Matt or you. Hell, Marco had to get a paternity test to prove he was Jess's father. It was a mess."

"I wasn't in the hospital anymore. By then I was in foster care." I hug him closer, realizing how lucky we are to be here, alive.

"I love you, Noah." But it means so much more than those simple words.

"I love you too, Lexi. Forever."

I fall asleep in the arms of the only man I've ever loved, a man I thought had given up on me. Who I'd almost given up on. Holding on to him now, it doesn't seem fair; I wish Marco could have had this. I wish he and Elise had gotten their happily ever after.

SIXTEEN

I offer to babysit Jess tonight for a fun girls' night with her, Bex, and me. Taking a batch of chocolate chip cookies out of the oven, I place them on the cooling rack. I've been baking and preparing all day, and I think I'm ready to host a child for the evening. I'm nervous about her coming here. What if she doesn't like me?

I don't have any more time to obsess because the door opens and Jess bolts inside excitedly.

"Auntie Lexi, I'm staying the night for real?"

"For real, sweetheart. Just us girls. No stinky boys allowed."

This gets a squeal and victory dance of epic cuteness.

Marco and Noah walk in behind her, carrying

more stuff than any five-year-old needs for one night away. The sight of it causes me to laugh out loud. "You sure you packed everything?" I ask cheekily. The doubt on Marco's face has me cracking up again. "I'm kidding! Here, let me help you into the guest room."

"Thanks. I always get a bit crazy when she's away from me, even for a night," he admits nervously.

"Don't worry, she'll be fine. Won't you, Miss Jess?"

"Yes, ma'am. We'll have so much fun, Daddy, don't worry," Jess says, reassuring her father with a hug and pat on his scruffy cheek, which has to be the sweetest thing I've ever seen.

"I'll help Marco set her stuff up," Noah says, kissing my cheek before disappearing down the hallway.

I turn the TV on for Jess while I tidy up my baking disaster in the kitchen.

"Ugh! I hate men. They're these wussy bastards who follow me around asking to buy me drinks, telling me I'm so pretty. Makes me sick. Like I would ever bang a guy in exchange for an appletini," Bex announces when she walks in, throwing her purse on the couch, next to Jess. Her eyes get real big and she swivels to me. "There's a small person on our couch."

"We're watching Jess tonight for Marco."

"Why? Does he have a date?" she asks, unable to hide the way her voice turns high-pitched and nervous. I have a feeling she likes Marco, but the two of them argue more than they flirt.

"Why, princess, you jealous?" Marco questions from behind her.

"Oh, hi, Marco. Nice to see you again," she says, smiling seductively while reaching her hand out to him, batting her eyes and biting her lip. This girl has no self-control.

"Keep it in your pants, princess. My daughter is sitting right there."

She looks confused that he isn't falling to his knees like most men do with her. "And you're just going to leave her here? What kind of man leaves his daughter with strangers so he can go hook up?"

"Woman, I can't even begin to tell you how wrong you are," he says with a shake of his head, looking at her like she's crazy. But the smile on his face tells me he kind of likes it. "Number one, Lexi is family to me and Jess's godmother. She isn't a stranger. And number two, you wouldn't know a good man if he clubbed you over the head and dragged you back to his cave."

"Woman? Woman! You're such a caveman. Who the hell do you think you are speaking to me like that?"

Marco steps into her face, whispering against her lips, "I could be your happily ever after, but you're too stubborn to pull your head out of the clouds long enough to actually see me."

I try to stifle my gasp. She just stares at him in shock; no guy has ever spoken to her like that. Most fall at her feet but end up being jerks.

I turn away and busy myself in the kitchen when he steps forward, pressing his lips against hers. My heart is happy at the new development, but I want to give them their moment. His kiss seems to stun Bex into silence.

"That's better," he says with a smirk, then turns, kisses Jess, and walks out the door with Noah, calling back, "Later, baby girl."

"Later," Bex says dreamily, not realizing until she hears the giggling that he was saying that to Jess.

Bex collapses on the couch next to Jess. "I sure like your daddy, kiddo."

Jess rolls her eyes. "Lots of skanks like him. Uncle

Noah says Daddy should steer clear of skanks. Are you a skank?"

Bex gasps in offense. "I most certainly am not. You're like three. Where did you learn that word?"

"I'm *five*."

"Your daddy has a lot of tattoos."

Jess crosses her arms, getting visibly upset. "So?"

"Has your daddy ever been in prison?"

"Bex!" I interject. What is she doing?

"No he hasn't! Have you?" Jess counters. I chuckle at her defending her daddy.

"No. Does he go on lots of dates?"

"No. But you probably do."

"What can I say? You gotta kiss a lot of frogs," she admits with a sigh.

Jess giggles. "Eww. You're not supposed to kiss frogs." She pauses, considering her words carefully. "Do you know how to make chocolate cake?"

"Yes, as a matter of fact, I do," Bex answers, obviously curious where this line of questioning is going.

Jess nods. "Good. Daddy likes chocolate cake. You could make him one, with sprinkles."

Bex gives Jess the side-eye. "I'll think about it."

"You do that. He says Mama made good chocolate cake. He fell in love with her with his tummy. Mama's an angel now."

"My mama died when I was little too."

Jess's face falls. "She's in heaven?" Tears form in her sweet blue eyes.

"Aw, honey, I'm sorry. I didn't mean to upset you."

She shrugs her little shoulders. "Daddy says I'm lucky. Not every girl has an angel for a mama."

"Your daddy sounds pretty perfect."

Jess gives a tiny sigh. "He's the best daddy ever."

I watch the sweet exchange from the kitchen before saying, "All right, you two. Are you ready for girls' night? We'll do our hair, have a fashion show, eat sweets, and watch a movie. Sound good to you, Miss Jess?"

"Yes!"

The night progresses with a lot of laughs, and we end the evening by watching a few Disney princesses. Bex and Jess develop a special bond, and we fall asleep on the pallet of blankets we made on the living room floor.

Sleeping on the hard floor seemed like a good idea until I wake up this morning with a backache. I sit up and see Jess curled into Bex, who has her arms around the sweet girl, like she's shielding her from the world. The image of it makes my heart swell. It's so beautiful.

Trying to be as quiet as possible, I sneak ou the room and grab my camera, never one to le a great photo op go to waste. They stir after about ten shots, so I sneak away into the kitchen to start a pot of coffee and gather ingredients for pancakes.

SEVENTEEN

My show, Healing Ink, opens with huge success. All my friends rally to support me on my special night. This is the first time I turned the camera on myself. My scars and tattoos are displayed on the walls alongside the rest of my subjects. I've never bared myself in this way, and it feels oddly empowering.

Life is good, calm, and, above all, happy. We've settled into a life of laughs and love. Lana and John have quickly adopted Jess into the family, spoiling her and spending as much time with her as they can before their next adventure calls.

Noah is helping me clear the table one night when he says, "Move in with me."

"What? Are you serious?" I bite my bottom lip in thought. "I don't know, Noah. I'm worried about ditching Bex. We've been each other's rock since I moved in with her and Lana. I feel awful thinking about leaving her on her own."

"Babe, we aren't leaving the country. I live ten minutes away."

"With Marco and Jess. How is that going to work? Are we going to move in with them? Maybe you could move in here?"

He smiles at that. "You'd be okay with that?"

"Of course! I hate the nights you sleep at your place. But doesn't he rely on you to help out with Jess?"

"Why don't we talk to them about it and see where they stand? I can still help with Jess from here."

I nod. "I've got to get ready to meet Sarah and Bex, babe. I'll talk to Bex tonight and call you when I get home."

"That place is full of douchebags trying to cop a feel."

"Aw, does my caveman hate when other guys look at his toy?" I joke. He just looks disgruntled thinking about me going out tonight. I smooth out his crinkly forehead, kissing the stress lines away. "It's one night out. It's the end of an era. We'll be fine. I still know how to kick some ass if need be." I wink.

"Sorry, babe. I'm not trying to control you. I just worry about you being around so many drunk assholes."

"I kicked your ass once, remember? I'm not as helpless as you think. I'm super scrappy," I say, pretending to box him.

He laughs and hugs me close. "I forgot about the beating you gave me. Marco bugged me about that for weeks."

"Love you. I'll call you when I get home," I say, kissing him goodbye.

A COUPLE HOURS INTO OUR GIRLS' NIGHT, Christopher the douche walks up to the bar. "Congratulations on your show's success. I heard it was impressive." He's swaying slightly, making him appear every bit the drunken fool he is. "Wanna come home with me to celebrate, sexy Lexi?"

I turn him down again, resisting the urge to rebreak his nose. "Not if you were the last man on earth. I broke your fricking finger and nose on our first date. What makes you think I would give you a second chance?"

As I turn my back to walk away, he grabs my arm, his fingers digging in painfully. I call Jimmy, the security guy, who happily drags Christopher out of there screaming.

"Lord, that man is a dick," Bex says once he's out of view.

"He's a loser. Moving on!" I call out to her as I shimmy away to the music and take the shot Sarah passes me.

The night feels like it goes on for days, and my feet are killing me. I find a quiet moment to give Bex the heads-up about Noah wanting to move in together, but in our inebriated state, we don't do much planning other than declaring our love for one another.

At the end of Sarah's shift, I call a cab to collect us.

Bex decides to stay behind with Sarah, waiting for Jimmy to be finished so she can catch a ride with him. I kiss them all goodbye and walk outside to wait for my cab. The cool air feels amazing after being in the stuffy club all night.

After a moment, gravel crunches beside me, sending chills down my spine.

I turn to see Christopher waiting for me. I roll my eyes at him swaying as he stalks toward me. "Go home, Christopher. I'm tired as hell and in no mood to deal with your crap. Leave now or I'll call the cops."

His fist comes out of nowhere, connecting with my jaw. Pain erupts across my face as I collapse, my knees hitting the sharp gravel. He punches me twice more before screaming, "You're always teasing me, parading your ass in front of me, laughing at me! You think I'm a joke." His hand closes around my throat, and I can't breathe.

In a daze, I pull at his hands, but my head is spinning. He pushes me back into the gravel, every rock cutting into me. He frantically and clumsily starts pulling at my clothes. "You made me do this."

Flashes of my attack bombard me until I find strength in myself. I refuse to be a victim again. I put my training to use once more, and I fight back with everything I have and manage to knock him off balance.

Quickly scrambling to my feet, I run for the club door, screaming, hoping someone hears me. I almost make it, but he tackles me to the ground again, my head cracking against the gravel.

As he turns me onto my back, I see the rage

twisting his face into something that will haunt me forever. When his weight presses me into the stones, I frantically scratch every inch of exposed skin I can access. He grabs my hand, wrenching it in his vise-like grasp, twisting it away from him and pinning it to the ground. I thrash and squirm beneath him, doing everything I can to avoid having my other hand pinned as well. It's not enough though. Too quickly, he has both hands grasped in one of his, and I can feel his erection press against my core.

I let loose a scream as loud as I can.

I hear a yelled "What the fuck!" from behind us, and his weight is suddenly lifted off me. I roll onto my side and throw up the contents of my stomach. I can't see straight; my head is pounding from too much alcohol and the beating I just took. I hear screaming and yelling from somewhere beside me, but I can't seem to make out the words.

"Baby, look at me. Are you okay?"

"Noah?" I start crying at the sound of his voice. He saved me. I try to stay awake, but I slip into blackness.

I SUFFERED A CONCUSSION AND AM BRUISED AND battered all over my body. The police came and arrested Christopher. Noah was livid that I walked out there alone at night and that security allowed it. And that I didn't tell him that Christopher had attacked me once before. Oops. I can tell he blames himself when I see him in the hospital. He collapses beside me and cries. We both do; tonight was too real, too much like the night we lost each other.

"I wish I'd been stronger, been able to protect myself," I sob.

"This isn't your fault. You did great. That bastard will get what he deserves."

"I love you."

"Marry me."

His words come as a complete shock, and it takes me a moment to register what he's said.

"No, not like this. The only reason you're asking me is because I'm all beat up and fragile."

"You know that's not true. I wanted to marry you the moment I saw you at King of Hearts. Hell, I wanted to marry you when you were a shy hot mess on a step and shocked the hell out of me when you kissed me. If you won't marry me yet, then at least move in with me. I need you close. I'm done being separated from you."

"Okay," I say with a crooked smile. My lip is split and swollen; I look like I lost a fight with a beehive.

We become inseparable from that point on, and when I'm given the okay to go home, Noah and I decide it's time to sit down with Bex and Marco and figure out our future. We've waited long enough.

"Why don't I take Noah's room at Marco's house?" Bex blurts, leaving us all in shock.

I glance at Marco, and he has a smile on his face like he just won the lottery. *What is going on with these two?* I think it's a huge disaster, but she and Marco assure me it's a great idea and that there's nothing going on. Resisting calling them out on their bull-shit, I stay quiet, curious how this will play out.

"If you're both sure this is what you want…."

"We're grown-ups, Lexi. I think we can handle it. And I can be there if he needs help with Jess."

With everyone in agreement, we plan on swapping Noah's and Bex's stuff the following weekend.

THANKSGIVING COMES, AND EVERYONE GETS together at our place for dinner. I'm all healed up now and am puttering around the kitchen with Lana and Bex.

Lana catches me staring off into the distance, thinking. "Penny for your thoughts, love."

I smile at her; she's so caring. "I've spent plenty of Thanksgivings in my life alone, never having a family who cared. Sometimes I want to pinch myself. I have this amazing group of people who I love and who love me. I feel so blessed."

"But… Matthew is missing?"

She knows me so well. "Yeah." I sigh. "I wish I knew where he was, that he was safe and loved."

"Patience, my dear. He'll find his way to you when he's ready. He may be hard to find, but you're not. You've left a trail of breadcrumbs leading straight to you. Now you have to wait for the universe to lead him to you."

It always comes back to fate and the universe with Lana. At first it seems so ridiculous, but after years of listening to her, I see its merit.

That night before bed, I close my eyes and send a silent prayer out into the universe for Matty to find his way to me. I've tried looking myself and hiring PIs, but now it's time for the universe to do its magic. I refuse to believe my brother is lost forever.

AFTER DINNER, WE HEAD DOWN TO THE BEACH TO watch the sunset and so Jess can run off some energy. Lana and John lay out a blanket, snuggling close. They're watching Marco and Bex chasing Jess in the waves a little way down the beach. Noah takes my hand and leads me to the water's edge. He seems preoccupied.

"You all right?" I ask, touching his cheek.

He smiles down at me, kissing my palm. "Better than okay. It feels like a dream, being together like this. I never thought…." Tears form in his loving eyes.

"Hey, no tears. This is a happy day. We found each other. That's all that matters."

Noah drops to his knees in front of me. "Lexi, I believe in miracles, and us finding each other was the greatest miracle in my life. Will you marry me?"

I burst into tears, dropping to the ground with him and crying, "Yes!"

Here, on our beach at sunset, all my dreams come true.

"I want to spend the rest of my life making miracles with you. I wish I could have been by your side all these years."

"You were with me though. I never lost sight of the life I wanted. I always knew that somehow I would find you. I think I needed that time we spent apart to heal myself. To get the help I needed to feel whole."

By the time we pick ourselves up off the sand and join the rest of the group, they're cheering in celebration for us. A perfect end to a perfect day, and we have so much to be thankful for.

EIGHTEEN

While I'm reorganizing my gallery, the bell over the door startles me out of my daydreaming. "Be right with you," I call out before finishing adjusting the frame on the wall.

"I'm not going anywhere. Take your time, sis."

My heart stops in my chest at those words. I turn around and come face-to-face with my brother. I burst into tears and run into his arms. We stand there clinging to each other for a few moments before I can form words and take a minute to look at him.

Six long years since I've seen his handsome face. He looks so different.

I lock up the gallery and lead him into the house. I can't help but stare at him as I put on a pot of coffee. "How did you find me? I looked for you for years. I thought I'd lost you forever."

"I looked for you too, but I didn't know where you were taken. I'm so sorry, Alexa. I brought those men into our lives. I was a mess back then, high all the time. Doing anything I could to make money: sell drugs, steal cars, fight. I owed the wrong guy. He found me that night and beat the crap out of me. I woke up in a hospital bed, beaten and bloody. When I got home, there was a bloody mess behind police tape, and you were gone. All I knew was two girls were shot and one was DOA. One shooter was killed by cops and one found dead in our apartment. Two men were taken into custody.

"I was a mess for a long time after that day. I looked for you but didn't know where to start. Fearing the worst, that you had been killed by the men I brought to our doorstep, I decided the only thing left to do was go to the cops myself and demand answers." He laughs. "What a stupid idea that was. Turns out I had an outstanding warrant, so when I barged into the cop shop, high as a kite, confronting them about that day, I was arrested and did six months in jail."

"Oh, Matty. Six months!" My heart sinks at the thought of him in jail.

"It was probably the best thing that ever happened to me. When I got out, I knew I wanted to change my life, but I was lost and without any family to lean on. I knew if I stayed where I was, I would cave and fall back into the life. Then one day I walked past a recruiter's office, and oddly enough, I liked what he had to say. I needed structure in my life, needed to learn to be a man, so I enlisted and spent the next couple years overseas. Two tours in Afghanistan."

I shudder at the thought of him dying in some godforsaken war and never seeing him again.

"It was the best decision I've ever made. And, well, it's also how I met my wife."

"You're married? Oh, Matty, I'm so happy. When can I meet her?"

"Soon. I came alone this trip, but next time I'll definitely be bringing them."

"Them?" I ask.

He pulls something out of his pocket and holds it out for me to see. "This is Cara, my wife, and Marshall, our son. He just turned two last month."

I cry happy tears over his picture. "What a lovely family you have. I can't wait to meet them." His son looks like a clone of Matty as a child.

"Why is the gallery locked up, babe?" I hear Noah

coming up the steps. When he sees Matty, I can tell it takes him a moment to figure out who he is. "Matt? Jesus, it's good to see you, man."

Matty gets up and gives him a man hug, each of them slapping the other on the back. "Great to see you're still looking out for her after all these years."

"Actually, we only found each other a few months back."

"How long can you stay for?" I ask my brother.

"I gotta get back as soon as possible, but this was the first solid lead I've had in years, so I had to come see for myself," he says, pulling me to his side. I wrap my arm around his waist and grin like a fool.

He stays for a few hours, meeting Bex, Marco, and Jess before he has to head back home, but not before promising to bring the whole gang back for Christmas in a few weeks.

I hug him so tight, not wanting him to leave but knowing he has a life to get back to. "I'm being ridiculous, but I hate letting you go."

"I'm not going anywhere, kid. It's been a long search, and now that I've found you and know you're safe and happy, I can go back home and relax for the first time in years."

We laugh and hug again before he has to leave to catch his flight home.

"Love you, big brother. Squish my nephew and sister-in-law for me."

"See you in a few weeks, Matt," Noah adds.

As we watch the cab pull away, Noah wraps his arms around me from behind. "Just when you think life can't get any more incredible."

I smile up at him. "It's a magical life, isn't it?"

"Yeah, babe, it really is."

CHRISTMAS IS WONDERFUL. THE HOUSE HAS decorations covering every surface. I must admit, since moving in with Lana and Bex, I've been a little crazy when it comes to Christmas, wanting everything to be perfect, especially this year. The tree is bursting at its seams with presents for everyone. The turkey is in the oven, smelling delicious already. Trays of treats are set out on every table.

"Babe, you've made enough food to feed an army," Noah says, snatching a candy cane-shaped cookie off the tray I'm adjusting for the tenth time.

"It needs to be perfect. Stop eating! Now the tray looks lopsided." I smack his hand, then adjust the cookies to hide the empty spot he left.

Wrapping his arms around my waist, he kisses

my neck. "I love this side of you. I can't wait until it's our kids you're obsessing over. But you really need to relax." He continues kissing up my neck until he hits that magical spot that makes my knees go weak and a moan slip out.

"Noah, they'll be here any minute," I murmur. "We don't have time."

"Challenge accepted," he says before throwing me over his shoulder and running upstairs to our bedroom. I'm so worked up it doesn't take either of us long before we're running for the door, laughing and readjusting our clothes on the way.

Bex walks in, and one glance at us has her laughing and rolling her eyes. "Merry Christmas, sinners," she whispers as she passes me.

I smack her and give Marco and Jess a hug, wishing them Merry Christmas. Jess gives me a quick hug before running to the Christmas tree and looking through the gifts to see which ones have her name on them.

Having Jess and Marshall, Matty's boy, here has made it so much more special. Everyone I love is gathered around the table.

Matty's wife, Cara, is the sweetest woman. She's visibly nervous when they first get here, holding on to Marshall because he's shy of all the new people, but it doesn't take long for her bright personality to shine through. I adore her instantly, watching her dote on Matty and their son. I want to sweep little Marshall up in a hug and squish him, but I'm a stranger to him, so I reluctantly bide my time and do my best to show him how awesome Auntie Lexi is while he's here.

Jess is great with him. She's his cheerleader and entertainment committee, showing him where we keep the toys and cookies. He loves her as much as we do after ten minutes in her presence, and it brings me to tears.

I've been an emotional wreck all day. I can't seem to stop myself from tearing up every five minutes from happiness. Lana bumps shoulders with me as we stand watching Jess and Marshall enjoy the chaos of gift opening. "I'm so happy for you, Lexi. This moment is everything you've ever wished for. I can feel happiness radiating off you in waves."

"The home you gave me and the love you showed me made this possible. I'll forever be grateful for that and the room to find myself. I love you, Lana."

"Aw, I love you too, sweetheart."

We turn our attention to Bex and Marco teasing each other, but there's something in their eyes that tells me there's much more there under the surface.

Lana nods in their direction. "What's that all about?"

I shrug in response, shaking my head. "I doubt they even know."

They've been doing this crazy dance around each other, clearly driving each other nuts in all kinds of ways. I'd say them moving in together was a terrible idea, but the way they bicker seems to be some kind of foreplay with them. It's bizarre to watch, like I'm a voyeur.

"One day soon, those two are going to explode and rip each other's clothes off," Lana says to me quietly.

I snicker, agreeing 100 percent.

Jess is playing with Marshall. She's being a bit of a diva but nothing too out of line, just regular strong-willed type of behavior. I can't help but notice she's starting to act a little like Bex, and I see Elise in her as well. It's sweet. The three of them make a cute little family. I bet Elise is looking down on them and smiling.

———

A FEW DAYS BEFORE MY WEDDING, I DECIDE TO finally go to Elise's grave with Marco, Jess, and

Noah. They go every month, but I just haven't been able to bring myself to, thinking it's just a headstone and I won't feel any different. Now, walking toward her grave, emotions are clogging my throat, making it hard to breathe. My soul aches for my best friend. For Jess's mom, for Marco's first love, for Noah's sister. Fat tears stream down my cheeks. It's too much of a tragedy; she deserved to live a long happy life. She meant so much to us, and her absence is felt every day. I'm a mess.

Little Jess is quite the opposite, light and carefree as she dances between headstones humming a little song. When we get to Elise's grave, Jess changes out the old flowers for new ones and brushes leaves off her mom's grave. All the while she natters on and on to Elise about the fascinating things she's seen and done since their last visit.

I let them have their time, and when they walk back to the car, I'm a bit relieved that they're giving me some time alone with her. I stand there awkwardly for a few seconds, not sure where to begin and feeling weird talking aloud.

"Hi, Elise. It's taken me a long time to find you." I don't know what to say, so I sit on the grass next to her headstone, letting the tears fall until it comes to me. "You saved my life that day, and so many times since." I brush my fingers over her name. "Jess is perfect. She's so much like you, but I guess you already know that, huh? I'm so glad I found all of you. I wish I could see you one last time to tell you how sorry I am for going back to my apartment that day. If I had only listened to you—" I break down, sobbing.

Arms wrap around me. "You know she'd kick your ass for blaming yourself. None of it was your fault."

I cry into Noah's arms for a few minutes. Once I've pulled myself together, he guides me back to the car, where Jess looks at me with huge tears pooled in her sweet blue eyes. In the car, she holds my hand on the ride home. "Don't be sad, Auntie Lexi. Mama would be so happy to see you."

This kid.

I pull her as close as I can and kiss her head. "You're right, sweetheart. I'll try."

Life is too wonderful to feel anything but love and happiness. Noah's right. Elise wouldn't want me to wallow. She would want me to dance in the rain and laugh every day. For her, I'll try.

NINETEEN

BREATHE IN... AND BREATHE OUT. I KEEP MY EYES closed as I let the sun warm my skin. *Just keep breathing.*

"Today is a dream come true." Lana gushes over me, tears in her eyes. She fiddles with my hair for the millionth time in the last twenty minutes. She's visibly excited about today, but then so am I.

Bex is watching me cautiously, making sure I'm okay. "You know you have nothing to be nervous about, right?"

"I know, Bex. I'm okay. Better than okay." I can't stop smiling. I'm marrying Noah King today.

After a chaotic three weeks of planning, our wedding day has finally arrived.

Everything is set up on the beach we sat on,

making plans for our future, so many years ago, the coordinates etched on our skin guiding our way back here.

The wide, endless blue sky stretches out above us as we stand with our family around us. A handful of people on a beach. Perfection. Neither of us wanted anything fancy, just a simple, elegant, and lovely ceremony with those people who mean the world to us. Our new family, celebrating two people who are truly meant for each other.

The weather is flawless as always, and as the sun begins to set, I know it's time. So much perfection wrapped up in this incredible day.

The sun is descending, cascading streaks of brilliant color across the sky. It's the perfect background to our vows. Paper lanterns light the whole area up in a golden hue with pops of orange and red accents throughout. The beauty of it all takes my breath away.

I settled on a simple white lace dress, formfitting in the bodice and flowing beautifully to my bare feet. I wanted my toes in the sand today, fancy wedding dress be damned. No one was going to fight the bride on this little detail. With my arm looped in John's, we walk out onto the beach, toward Noah and our future together.

Little Jess walks ahead of us in her sparkly pale pink dress, laying flower petals at her feet in such a serious and delicate manner; you can tell she's taking her flower girl job very seriously. Marshall acts as our ring bearer, standing in front of where Matty and Cara are seated. Both little ones are doing a great job considering this has to be boring to a child.

With our family and friends circled around us, we vow to love and protect each other from this day forward. We spend the evening under a million twinkly lights, laughing and dancing our night away. It is the single most perfect day of my life.

How did I get here? How do all my dreams lie at my feet after years of wanting? I keep reminding myself that this isn't a dream, that I am now Lexi King.

My heart is giddy.

A FEW DAYS LATER, WE'RE PACKING FOR THE honeymoon—Marco booked us a bungalow right on the beach for a week as a wedding present. Noah has to run to the shop to finish up his last tattoo before we head out, which works out perfectly because I need to swing by Bex and Marco's house to coerce her into lending me her flowery beach wrap. Jess is at school when I arrive, but I hear a ruckus coming from somewhere in the back of the house.

"Hey, Bex, I need, like physically *need*, to borrow your beach wrap for the honeymoon. I can't find mine, and we leave tomorrow morning," I say as I walk into her bedroom—where I come face to… not exactly face with a very naked Marco and Bex. I scream bloody murder and run out screaming, "My eyes, I'm blind. Oh my God! Marco, stop touching my sister!"

I can hear Marco swearing and Bex laughing as I assume they're righting themselves before having to face me. Everything between those two is a powder keg. I knew this was going to happen, no matter how many times she assured me they weren't banging.

"Grow up, Lexi. It's sex. You're a married woman now. I'm sure you know what it is," Marco states with an eye roll as he steps into the kitchen, throwing a shirt on as he approaches.

"I knew this would happen when she moved in here, I just didn't expect to get a front row seat."

Bex slinks out, looking guilty, like her mom caught her making out on the couch. She tosses the beach wrap at me. "Keep it. It looks better on you anyway."

"No need to bribe me, Bex. I love you both. I'm happy for you. And I will keep it, thanks," I say, sticking my tongue out. I really am happy for them. I knew there was something going on with them, but neither mentioned it, so I assumed it was private. Inside, I do a little happy dance. "Two of my favorite people have found each other and are going to get married and have lots of babies," I exaggerate excitedly just to annoy them.

Their response is perfection as they both groan, "Ugh, shut up," and "Jesus, woman, what is wrong with you?"

I laugh all the way to my car. This is going to be fun.

I beeline for Noah's shop, eager to tell him what I found. I'm giggling to myself as I walk into his office, still not believing what I saw.

"What are you laughing at?" Noah asks, walking over to kiss me.

"I just busted Bex and Marco naked."

Laughing, Noah says, "Ha! I knew it! They were acting weird at the reception. It's going to be fun torturing them."

"We can tease them when we get back. It's honeymoon time, baby."

Noah leans over, planting a kiss on my lips.

"*Naked* honeymoon time."

"I won't be naked all the time."

He groans. "Stop killing the dream, babe. Let's go before you get any other crazy ideas."

A MONTH OR SO AFTER OUR WEDDING, I GET AN EMAIL from Matty. He's heard about a job opening on a base nearby and is trying to swing a transfer but tells me not to get my hopes up because these things take time. With luck he'll be moving to Cali next year. He'll still be a couple hours away, but just knowing I could hop in my car and see them makes my heart happy. I've been messaging Cara and we get along well. She has the best sense of humor, and I adore her and Marshall.

Since the wedding, Noah and I have settled into our blissful little lives together happily. What more could I ever want or need?

A baby perhaps?

Because that's what the two lines on the test I have clenched in my hand is telling me. I'm pregnant —and freaking the hell out because we only just got home from our honeymoon. We've only been married a hot minute.

So I do what I always do when the world feels like it's closing in on me: I call Lana and ask her to come over for tea. I need to talk this out with her before I lose my mind.

After I've got her seated at the table with a teacup in her hands, she begins. "So, what's got you in a panic?"

"I'm pregnant," I blurt.

She jumps out of her seat, squealing and hugging me. After a moment, when she realizes I'm not as gleeful, her face turns somber and she sits back down. "Why aren't you happy? You found the man of your dreams, against all odds, got married, and are expecting. That sounds like a damn fairy tale, not something to be sad about. What's going on in that head of yours?"

"What if I end up ruining this child like I was ruined? What if I'm not strong enough?"

"You're going to be a brilliant mother, and you have us to lean on when you have a bad day." She takes my face in her hands so I'm looking directly into her eyes. "Don't be scared, my dear. Tell Noah, let him ease your fears."

"You're right, as always. I don't know why I panicked. It's just... I never imagined any of this was possible a short time ago. It's all happening so fast."

"When the universe hands us our dreams, we don't ask why. We smile and hold that dream close."

With Lana's help, I realize that no matter how we're raised, what kind of damage was done to us, we can grow and become better than our parents.

"Just because you were raised in hell doesn't mean you can't give love. No one is perfect, Lexi, but the love you can offer a child is limitless. You'll be an amazing mother. I'm so proud of the woman you've become."

"Thank you, Lana. I couldn't have done it without you."

"I'm going to be a grandma!" Lana shouts at the same time Bex says from where she was standing in the doorway, "I'm going to be an auntie?"

"You sneaky cow!" I stick my tongue out at her, then grin. "Well, I guess since the cat's out of the bag, I'd better tell Noah. Do you think he'll be excited?"

"Of course he will," Bex assures me. We share a hug and make plans to go baby shopping.

Once I've calmed down, I realize this isn't the end of the world—it's the beginning of a whole new life. I'm married and having a baby with the love of my life.

Now I just need to tell Noah.

TWENTY

WHY AM I SO NERVOUS? I KNOW NOAH LOVES ME AND will love our baby with his whole heart, but there's still that awful voice in my head. I've spent my entire life trying to fight against that voice, the one telling me I'm not good enough.

I take a deep breath, locking away my doubt and focusing on telling Noah the good news.

"What's all this?" he asks when he sees the candles and picnic I arranged. Am I making way too big a deal out of this?

I walk over to greet him with a kiss. "It's silly, but I wanted to do something special today. How was work?"

"Good, busy. How was your day?"

"I didn't get much work done, but I had Lana over for tea and Bex stopped by."

He tilts his head, looking at me curiously. "What happened? You only have tea with Lana when you need her advice. Are you okay?"

I step up on my toes, wrapping my arms around his neck, kissing him. Like ripping a Band-Aid off, I say, "I'm pregnant."

He gasps against my lips. "Really?"

I nod as a tear slips down my cheek. I'm so emotional today. "You're going to be a daddy, Noah."

He picks me up and swings me around, laughing. Stopping abruptly, he drops to his knees in front of me, placing his hands on my stomach. "I'm going to spoil you so hard, kiddo," he says before lifting my shirt and planting a kiss below my belly button, sending a shiver through my whole body. He looks up at me with a brilliant smile. "I love you, Lexi."

"I love you too," I say before dropping to the floor and kissing him with all that I am.

"That was one hell of a honeymoon," he says with a chuckle and a smug look.

I can't help but laugh and roll my eyes.

· · ·

WITH THE WHOLE FAMILY GATHERED THAT SUNDAY for dinner, we share our news, which is, of course, greeted with hugs and congratulations.

"Nice work on the honeymoon, Noah," Marco says, earning him a fist bump.

"Oh my God, what is it with guys? They act like they built a house."

"Better, he built a baby!" His comment earns him a high five from Noah and an eye roll from me. These two, they're giant children.

Matty and Cara couldn't make it, but we video chat with them, letting them know a niece or nephew is on the way. He has tears in his eyes and congratulates us. I can't wait for them to move closer.

Sitting at the table, I look around at this family I built up out of nothing, a family that was scattered to the wind until, against all odds, we found our way back into each other's lives. They've become every-thing to me, and it makes my heart full just knowing they're in my life. I feel like my life is complete, personally and professionally.

Noah tucks me into his side, catching me watching Jess show everyone a magic trick. Lana has embraced the role of grandma to Jess, taking her for sleepovers once a month, and Jess is thriving having all us girls around. Poor thing has lived in an all-boys world for so long, so we're training her in the ways of the girl.

"I never knew life could be so fulfilling, so happy," I say, leaning my head on his shoulder.

"You deserve all the happiness in the world. You've shed enough tears for a lifetime. I plan on spending the rest of my life making sure your days are blissfully happy."

I smile up at him. "Mission accomplished."

EPILOGUE

I wake up gasping, cradling my swollen belly as it tenses and the baby rolls over inside. *What was that?* I breathe my way through the pain emanating through my middle.

Noah stirs beside me, resting a hand on my belly. "Are you okay? Is it time?"

"I think so, but I'm not sure." Slowing my breathing, I lie on my side facing him, the light from the windows shining in. It's morning, but just barely.

Noah sits up beside me, placing a hand on my belly.

"What if—" The baby rolls again, making me wince, and then the cramping starts up again. Something's wrong, I can feel it.

"Those were close together, babe. I think we should go to the hospital."

"Oh God, it's time. I have to call Lana, and Bex, and—"

"Babe. All you have to do is breathe. I'll call Marco, and he'll call the rest of the entourage. We have set everything up, and it's going to be okay."

I sit up in bed, clinging to my swollen belly. "Look at me," Noah says, touching my chin. I lock eyes with the man of my dreams, the father of my baby. "Everything will be okay." And I believe him. His certainty is shining through his dark eyes, and I can't help but smile.

"I love you, Noah."

"I love you too. Now let's get you ready," he says, reaching out his hands for me to take. At this phase of my pregnancy, I need his assistance to get to my feet.

The moment I stand up, warm water gushes between my legs. "Oh" is all I say, attempting to see over my belly to the puddle on the floor.

"Well, that escalated quickly." A smile plays on his handsome face. How is he not terrified? Right, because it's my vagina that's about to be destroyed. I cringe, remembering the birthing video I watched. So much screaming and pushing. "Lexi, I'll get the car ready. You call Marco and Bex. I'll be right back to help you get dressed, okay?" He places a phone in my shaky hands.

"How are you so calm?"

"Because by the end of this we'll have our baby in our arms. That's all that matters."

"Tell that to my vagina," I mumble, dialing my cell.

Bex answers the phone on the third ring, screaming, "Is it baby time?"

"Yes. We'll be going to the hospital soon. I need you to text everyone. We'll text as soon as we know what's happening."

She squeals into the phone so loud that I have to pull it away from my ear. "Baby time!"

The line goes quiet for a moment, and I croak, "I'm scared, Bex."

Her gasp is audible. "You're going to be amazing. You and Noah are the perfect parents, and this baby will be the world's most loved child that has ever existed, with a huge family showering it with love every day of its life. You hear me?"

"Yes, ma'am," I say with a smile. "I love you."

"Love you too. Okay, you go birth that sweet baby, and I'll call the cavalry and meet you there!"

I hang up as Noah walks in. "Everything's loaded. You get a hold of Bex?"

I nod, leaning my head against his chest. He rubs his hands down my back. Wrapping my arms around his neck, I gaze dreamily into his dark eyes and smile.

Today we become a family.

WHEN OUR BABY GIRL IS PLACED IN MY ARMS AND I lock eyes with her, I fall in love and everything clicks into place. The last piece of my heart is healed. Surrounded by my family, I'm finally whole.

It's been a long road here, but every bump, every dark twist and turn has led us here, the beginning of something so powerful. From the harsh exposure to the dark world to the overwhelming power of love. I feel complete now. Cradling this sweet baby in my arms, I know everything will be all right.

Love is worth all the pain and uncertainty I've experienced in my life. This moment, this is what it's all about. This moment is everything. With Noah by my side and my family around us for support, we can take on anything.

I used my past pain to empower me to keep going when it felt like the whole world was closing in on me, when everything seemed so dark and hopeless. All along, I kept a small flicker of hope alive that the universe would bring my family back. That one day the world wouldn't be so painful. That one day I too would get the happily ever after I deserved.

The universe is beautiful. Never forget that.

I HOPE YOU ENJOYED LEXI AND Noah's story. Be sure to check out *Kate* by Charyse Allan if you're looking for heat and gripping, heartbreaking romance.

Also check out Alim and Elaine's story, *The Misguided Confession*, if you're looking for a fresh shifter romance in a contemporary setting.

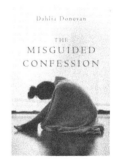

ACKNOWLEDGMENTS

Biggest thanks always goes to Kristian, my love. You are an amazingly supportive man, father, and husband, we are lucky to have you in our lives. Thank you for always being the glue that holds us all together.

Thank you, Crystal, for every single day you listened to me rant about all my doubts and told me to hush and keep writing. I appreciate your friendship more than you know.

Hot Tree group, you are an incredible group of brilliant women who have been my teachers and tribe in this crazy indie book world. Your support, editing knowledge, and general sass makes me smile daily and I love you all.

Thank you to the PLN girl gang, for your unwavering support and encouragement.

ABOUT THE AUTHOR

Born and raised in the Pacific Northwest in coastal British Columbia, Kolleen Fraser finds the lush green forests, snow-capped mountains, and the ocean waves soothing to her soul.

She's always been an avid reader and loves blogging about her favorite reads. Her writing journey began by hitting publish on her first novel in her duet in 2015. Since then, she's written across multiple romance genres.

Writing has always been therapeutic for Kolleen and offers a way to process and express all the crazy thoughts running around in her head while telling powerful stories in real ways that readers can connect with.

Newsletter: https://kolleenfraser.wordpress.com/contact/

facebook.com/AuthorKolleenFraser
twitter.com/KolleenWrites
instagram.com/KolleenWrites
bookbub.com/authors/kolleen-fraser

ABOUT THE PUBLISHER

Hot Tree Publishing opened its doors in 2015 with an aspiration to bring quality fiction to the world of readers. With the initial focus on romance and a wide spread of romance subgenres, Hot Tree Publishing has since opened their first imprint, Tangled Tree Publishing, specializing in crime, mystery, suspense, and thriller.

Firmly seated in the industry as a leading editing provider to independent authors and small publishing houses, Hot Tree Publishing is the sister company to Hot Tree Editing, founded in 2012. Having established in-house editing and promotions, plus having a well-respected market presence, Hot Tree Publishing endeavors to be a leader in bringing quality stories to the world of readers.

Interested in discovering more amazing reads brought to you by Hot Tree Publishing? Head over to the website for information:

www.hottreepublishing.com

facebook.com/hottreepublishing
twitter.com/hottreepubs
bookbub.com/profile/4135535500

CPSIA information can be obtained
at www.ICGtesting.com
Printed in the USA
BVHW081317180920
589008BV00002B/172

9 781922 359308